P.
BOO

Esther David writes about Jewi............ndia and personally illustrates
her books. She is the author of the highly acclaimed *The Walled City*,
Book of Esther, *Man with Enormous Wings* and *Ahmedabad: City
with a Past*, among others. She has also written a collection of short
stories, *By the Sabarmati*, a children's book, *My Father's Zoo*, and
co-authored *India's Jewish Heritage: Ritual, Art and Life-cycle*. Her
books have been translated into several languages, including French,
Gujarati and Marathi. Her work is included in the library of modern
Jewish literature, Syracuse University Press, New York.

Esther received the Sahitya Akademi Award for English literature
in 2010 and the Hadassah-Brandeis Institute Research Award, USA,
for documenting the Bene Israel Jews of Gujarat and the study of
Indo-Jewish cuisine. The French translation of *Book of Rachel*
received the Prix Eugénie Brazier. Esther belongs to the Bene Israel
Jewish community of Ahmedabad.

PRAISE FOR THE BOOK

'It is a raw mango of a book, as sweet and tart as the memories of an Indian childhood . . . to most people it would consist one portion of R.K. Narayan, the sheer exuberance of Malgudi, a dash of sentimentality from Tagore's "Kabuliwallah" . . . David uses the recipes she has garnered to tell Rachel's story with the same zest and involvement which Rachel employed to cook for her family'
—Geeta Doctor, *India Today*

'Both a gripping story and a chronicle of a unique community'
—*Deccan Chronicle*

'*Book of Rachel* is a touching and intimate story of a woman who preserves the heritage of memory and culture. The novel is about the old who have been left behind in India by families, which immigrated to Israel. Set in Danda, on the picturesque Konkan coast, Rachel's life revolves around her fight to preserve an ancient synagogue. She deals with the pervading sense of isolation, by trying out an ancient recipe every day. Rachel's story is woven around love, longing, recipes and the Jewish heritage in India'—citation for the Sahitya Akademi Award 2010

'This prize is given to Esther David; as her novel *Book of Rachel* celebrates the way she writes about love and food as well as pays tribute to her understanding of the link between cooking, traditions and transmission, as it is a touching and intimate story of a woman who preserves the heritage of memory and culture'—citation for Prix Eugénie Brazier, France (for the French translation)

BOOK *of*
RACHEL

Esther David

PENGUIN BOOKS

An imprint of Penguin Random House

PENGUIN BOOKS

USA | Canada | UK | Ireland | Australia
New Zealand | India | South Africa | China | Singapore

Penguin Books is part of the Penguin Random House group of companies
whose addresses can be found at global.penguinrandomhouse.com

Published by Penguin Random House India Pvt. Ltd
4th Floor, Capital Tower 1, MG Road,
Gurugram 122 002, Haryana, India

First published in Viking by Penguin Books India 2006
Published in Penguin Books by Penguin Random House India 2018

Text and illustrations copyright © Esther David 2006

10 9 8 7 6 5 4 3 2

ISBN 9780143444534

Typeset in Sabon by R. Ajith Kumar, New Delhi
Printed at Repro India Limited

www.penguin.co.in

To my granddaughter,
Mira-Rachel-Roma

Acknowledgements

At the age of seven, if grandmother Shebabeth had not forced me to cut frills around the kippur chi puri, had I not received Aunt Abigail Solomon's recipe book from cousin Elizabeth Elijah, had I not travelled to Alibaug and Danda to research for *Book of Esther* and discovered the small Jewish community, cooking in the traditional way, had I not written about a black sauce in *The Walled City*, not knowing what it meant, had I not read a clipping about another Rachel who spent a lifetime looking after a cemetery in Pakistan, had I not got involved with the Vadodara cemetery, had I not collected Jewish artefacts for Ahmedabad's city museum, had I not heard cousin Sybil David become nostalgic with details of some long-forgotten recipe, had I not remembered the fragrance of green coconut curry my mother, Sarah, used to make on Sundays and if Julie Pingle had not demonstrated the finer points of Bene Israel Jewish cooking while making the rose-coloured chik cha halwa, *Book of Rachel* would not have materialized.

I also acknowledge Namrata Dwivedi for researching and reading the text and Advocate Nilesh Trivedi for advising me on disputed religious sites, Lilaben and Raili for helping me make some recipes, Bijoy Shivram for images, Centre national du livre, Paris, for including 'Rachel', then a short story, in their anthology for Les Belles Étrangères – Inde, and Maison des Écrivains Étrangèrs et des Traducteurs, St. Nazaire France where I wrote a few chapters, Regine Herzberg Poloniecka, the other grandmother of my grandchildren, for cooking all those Polish Jewish dishes and inspiring me to discover the Indian tradition, my French translator-friend Sonja Terangle, for asking me so many questions about Bene Israel food, my daughter Amrita for trying out some recipes and making them better than me, my Penguin editors Krishan Chopra and Jaishree Ram Mohan for giving form to this novel and, finally, Amrita, my son Robin, son-in-law Nathaniel, grandchildren Kiran-Amos and Mira-Rachel-Roma, for being ever so appreciative about my Jewish cooking!

FRIED FISH

Ingredients: fish, salt, lemon, chilli powder, oil

Choose a big pomfret, according to the dietary law, a fish with scales, never without scales. Also, avoid a bruised fish. Pomfret is often pronounced as 'pamplet'.

Method: Gut fish innards. Remove tail, but keep head with eyes. Cut fish into five or six pieces. Rub lemon and salt. Keep aside. Wash, drain, dry and rub red chilli powder on fish pieces. Heat oil in a frying pan or iron griddle and fry fish on both sides, drain and serve hot, with slivers of lemon.

Fried fish is eaten as part of a meal, often with chapattis, or dal and rice.

❖❖

The fish is the symbol of protection, because she does not have eyelids and her eyes are always open and watchful, placed on both sides of her head. She is the protector of the home, like the woman of the house. A fish is portrayed on the ornamental hand sign seen in Jewish homes, the hamsas, for protection and good luck. A fish also signifies fertility because of the number of eggs she produces and is also linked to the zodiac sign of Pisces.

The cyclone lashed Rachel's house exactly at three thirty that afternoon and brought with it a fish at her doorstep. The fish was alive and lay there writhing and gasping for breath. It was a pomfret. Fresh, with pink fins, like the one that the fishmonger brought every Friday morning. Rachel would pick the best of the lot, press the white liquid from the fins to test its freshness, and then cut it into five or six pieces on the morli, her scythe-shaped metal chopper.

Touched with blood, the fish looked like the petals of the flame of the forest, which was in full bloom over her roof.

Fresh fish, fried with a generous sprinkling of fiery red chilli powder, had been Rachel's Sabbath dinner for years. In fact it was her weakness. Normally she would have accepted the fish that had come to her with the storm as a gift from the Lord, and eaten it for dinner, but today she did not.

Watching the waves from the Arabian Sea rise as high as the coconut trees, Rachel remembered the dark night when the Jews had been shipwrecked in India, in fact in this very sea.

She did not want the fish to die. The sea had given it to her. Rachel picked up the twitching fish in her hands and dropped it into the bucket of water she always kept in the veranda.

When it rained, Rachel collected precious rainwater to wash her brass pots. When she had nothing better to do, she sat in the drizzle, cleaning the brass with tamarind, hoping that the clouds would not part. If the sun appeared, the pots would lose their shine and turn bluish grey like the rain clouds.

Rachel was drenched. She removed her wet sari, dried it on a string and sat on her haunches watching the fish. She was shivering and everything around her seemed to be trembling like the fish in the bucket. The house was rattling and shaking as though it would collapse with the force of the wind. Brownie, the mongrel she had adopted, had curled up on a cushion under her bed, his ears twitching as he sensed there was a fish in the bucket.

With the onslaught of the rains, the goats had herded on to the veranda. She recognized the speckled one rubbing its body on the door. Rachel had pushed the poultry under a huge basket. Fluttering and dashing against each other, they were safer inside than outside. Unfortunately the basket was not big enough to accommodate the ducks. She had left them in the garden near the pond. But even they trooped in with the goats.

Rachel saw that the fish could not possibly swim in the bucket. It was not the sea. Rachel looked around for a larger pan, the type she had used to collect fodder when they had oxen. The pan was stored away on the mezzanine. She stepped on the ladder, but hesitated. Alone in the house, she did not like to climb ladders. She was always afraid of breaking her leg. If she were to be laid up, she would be at the mercy of others till her dying day.

She dreaded the day either her two sons or daughter would be forced to take her to Israel and admit her to a hospital and eventually abandon her in an old people's home. She did not like the idea. She was a free spirit; she needed to be in the land she had known, a land where her other half, Aaron, was buried, the familiar land which belonged to their forefathers. Whenever her sons and daughter spoke about her immigration to Israel, she shivered and imagined they would imprison her forever in an unknown land and tie her tongue with the language of their prayers.

She could hear the wind whistling around her and knew that a tree behind her house had fallen. The thunder sounded like gigantic cymbals, which were played during her eldest son's wedding.

Suddenly, she felt a strange sound inside her blouse. She cupped her breast with her hand and realized that it was her heart, beating like that of the fish she had held in her palms. She needed to be close to her youngest, Zephra.

Cyclones were not unusual in the Konkan, especially if you lived near the sea. She was afraid, not only for herself and the house but also for the synagogue. A few metres away from the house, it stood alone, distant and abandoned.

Rachel remembered that when Aaron was alive, every Friday for the Sabbath, she used to prepare a festive dinner, a coconut curry of chicken, mutton or fish, with mounds of steamed white rice. This tradition came to an end when Aaron died and the children left for Israel.

When Aaron died, she had wanted to jump into the sea and follow him. She had borne him two sons and a daughter. In between them, she had two miscarriages and an abortion. When the children had reached the age of eighteen or twenty, they had immigrated to Israel. All alone in the house, Rachel felt her life had no meaning.

In Israel the family was growing. Year after year, they visited her and tried to convince her to leave India and make a home with them in the Promised Land. Much to the amusement of the children and grandchildren, she would smile and say, 'Next year in Jerusalem.'

As a rule she spoke in Marathi, the language she had known since her birth. On one of their trips to India, when she heard her grandchildren speak in Hebrew, she smiled appreciatively and said, 'The Lord is great—the children speak in the language of the Torah.'

If for some reason the family could not come to India, they tried to entice her with descriptions of Israel. Rachel felt reassured that they had not forgotten Marathi when they spoke to her on the phone. And if the grandchildren spoke a few broken Marathi words, she was pleased.

Even Zephra always spoke to her in Marathi. She had left for Israel when she was in her teens and, having lived on a kibbutz, she behaved like an Israeli, much to Rachel's chagrin. Rachel was annoyed that Zephra refused to get married to one of the nice Bene Israel suitors one could still find in the south of Israel, Bombay or even Ahmedabad.

She had known her husband since she was a child. They were cousins and according to custom were married when they were in their teens. They had grown up together. They had spent a lifetime looking after each other's needs. And when Aaron died, Rachel did not know what to do with her life. She would often ask herself, how do you start doing things for yourself?

But then the people of the village had been caring and affectionate. They appreciated the fact that, although she was a Bene Israel Teli, she spoke Marathi with the right intonations, just like them, and also knew all the Maharashtrian customs, so much so that often they introduced her to their relatives as a Konkanasth Brahmin. Rachel took pride in her new-found identity, which made her a part of their lives, not a stranger who belonged to a minority community.

The way she dressed, behaved and spoke made it easier for them to accept her as one of them. Her neighbours had made it a habit to spend their afternoons with Rachel. They brought her food, knowing very well that sometimes Rachel skipped lunch or dinner.

She cooked for herself only on Friday, the Sabbath eve, perhaps fish or chicken and a goblet of the home-made sherbet for the Kiddush with a Sabbath bhakhri instead of bread.

The Bene Israel Jews observed the Sabbath from Friday evening to Saturday, which was one reason they were known as the Shanvar Telis of Danda. They had been oil traders by profession and always stopped work from Friday evening to Saturday evening.

Friday was the only day Rachel ate well and kept some food away for the next day's Sabbath lunch. Religiously on Friday afternoons, Rachel opened the ancient lock of the synagogue and oiled it so that it did not rust easily. Then, humming a Hebrew prayer in Marathi, she swept the floor, mopped it, wiped the chairs and saw to it that the synagogue was neat and clean. She believed that one day there would be a service and her efforts would not go to waste.

Rachel had spent a lifetime cooking for Aaron and the children. She had particularly enjoyed cooking for the festivals. And, she enjoyed serving the food. When Aaron insisted that she should sit down and eat with them, she scolded him, telling him not to rob her of simple pleasures. The only day they ate together was when they had had a fight and made up by feeding each other and eating from the same plate.

She kept herself busy, taking care of the abandoned synagogue. It stood at the back of the house. On lonely nights she felt comforted, watching its uneven silhouette from her window. The Grecian pillars and Ionic roof betrayed its majestic past. Through the years the fence dividing the space between the house and the synagogue had slowly broken down, giving the appearance that both stood on the same land. She was the last surviving Jew of Danda. For years the synagogue had been locked and when Jewish tourists from America or Israel visited the synagogue it was hard to open the lock and take them around the dusty synagogue. Over the years, the trustees of the synagogue had found it convenient to leave the synagogue keys with Rachel. She kept it clean and welcomed the occasional tourist, offering tea, limbu paani or lunch.

Rachel had sentimental attachments with the synagogue. She had been married here, her sons were circumcised here and they had all celebrated the festivals here. Her house being the closest to the synagogue, the traditional malida plates of flaked rice and fruit for the Eliyahu Hannabi prayers were always prepared there. That is, as long as there was a cantor and a minyan of ten men.

When the cantor left, they still had a minyan of ten men and Aaron continued to conduct the Sabbath services. From the fraternity of ten men, some died, others immigrated to Israel, and now the synagogue had no minyan, no cantor, no services.

In her solitude, Rachel had discovered many things about

herself. She preferred her fish fried, red and piping hot. She enjoyed eating an unusual combination of sticky rice and fried fish mixed with a sumptuous helping of ghee, although she had a vague idea that it was against the dietary law.

In the same way that she had become careless about her diet, she had also become careless about her saris. It took her some time to accept that she did not like the traditional nine-yard saris. She had stopped wearing them since Aaron died, and kept them stored away in a tin trunk. If someone asked her why she never wore them, she shrugged off the question with a vague answer that she had taken to wearing the modern five-yard saris.

But, often, as the Sabbath set on the Arabian Sea, she opened her trunks, picked up a nine-yard sari of her choice, draped it around her frail body and stood watching the sunset, whispering a silent prayer.

As she grew older, Rachel discovered that she liked the saris in pastel shades displayed at the Alibaug Sari Emporium. She liked the feel of the cool cottons and slippery synthetics in pale powder pinks, sky blues and mauves. And she fantasized about white saris with thin gold borders. The only dark colour she fancied was a deep aubergine.

As a rule, married women did not wear whites, but when Aaron was alive Rachel had convinced him to buy her one for the Yom Kippur prayers. Later, as a widow, she had worn white for a year or two and then switched to pastels.

Rachel often fretted that nobody was aware of her preferences, not even Aaron. The children had bought for her the best stainless steel vessels, plastic buckets, casseroles, silver and glassware. Yet, she was deeply attached to her copper and brass pans. Even if she did not use them, she kept them shining and silvered year around.

She had been deeply offended when her elder daughter-in-law had asked her to sell off her brass as it was of no use to anybody. She had replied rather tersely, 'I grew up with them; bury them with me.'

Watching the rain, Rachel was glad she had closed all the doors and windows of the synagogue. The latches and locks were old and strong; the doors and windows would not possibly fly open with the strong wind. But the roof was bad and there was one particular ventilator with a broken glass in the women's gallery through which the cyclonic winds could damage the synagogue.

Rachel remembered the Lord by chanting *Deva re Deva*. She hoped he would hear and help her in her hour of need. Humming the Marathi version of *The Lord is my shepherd*, she tried to light a candle. There was a power failure and she knew she would not have light for two days or more. Perhaps there would be power for a few hours, off and on, but it normally fluctuated during the monsoon.

Rachel checked her lanterns and made sure she had a good supply of kerosene in the house. She blessed her children; they had seen to it that the house had every possible gadget. She had a small cherry-coloured fridge, a leaf-green mixer, a new cooking range, two cylinders of cooking gas, a peacock-blue Formica-topped dining table, a sofa set with frills, steel cupboards, a two-in-one cassette player, a colour television and a white telephone from America. But when there was a power cut, none of the electric goods worked, only the cooking range and the hurricane lamp. She had become so used to the lantern that she often forgot that she had a torch, which she kept on the bedside table. She used it only when she had nightmares and felt the shadows of the trees were dancing around her.

Rachel saw the sky was overcast with dark clouds. It was four o'clock and she still had time to run down to the synagogue to have a look at the damage. She tied her sari around her bony legs, tied a plastic bag on her head, closed the door behind her, opened her big black umbrella and ran towards the synagogue.

Through the curtain of rain, in a sudden flash of lightning, it emerged like a grey, looming monument with a halo around it. The Hebrew lettering was washed clean on the marble plaque. The path was slushy and Rachel's legs were covered with mud when she reached the door. Soaking wet, she stood under the arched doorway, shut the umbrella and hurried over the brick steps leading to the entrance of the synagogue and stood there shivering like a wet sparrow.

She did not want to face the Holy Ark with her clothes sticking to her body. She had been taught that one should be dressed properly in a house of prayer. Rachel waited for a while in the veranda for the monsoon wind to dry her sari. She then covered her head with the end of her sari and entered the synagogue.

Rachel saw that the chandeliers and lamps were swinging dangerously with the strong wind from the broken ventilator. She rushed up to the ladies' gallery and saw that yet another glass window had broken and the floor was covered with fine shards of glass. Rachel hesitated. She looked down at her feet, thin, bony, sharp, discoloured nails, shaped like the claws of a bird.

She cursed herself for having left her chappals at home as it was easier to walk barefoot in the slush. She hopped on to the nearest bench and reached the ventilator. On the way she grabbed a laminated calendar of the Prophet Elijah.

A fresh onslaught of rain hit her face as she covered the ventilator with the calendar. She fixed it in place and returned, jumping over the benches. 'Nako baba,' she told herself, 'I don't want to hurt my feet for a holy cause.'

When she reached the door, Rachel realized she had forgotten to kiss the mezuzah. She returned and, profusely apologizing to the Lord, touched her fingertips to the marble surface and kissed it. Then covering herself with the end of her sari, she ran towards her house, holding on to the umbrella and hoping the cat had not eaten the fish.

She had forgotten to close the kitchen window.

SOL KADHI

Ingredients: coconut, wet cocum or mangosteen, rice, red chilli powder, turmeric, cumin powder, salt

Method: Choose a meaty coconut kernel with a hard outer nut. Shake it and listen for the sound of water in its belly. The outer covering of fibres should be removed with a sharp instrument. To break the coconut, one must hit its head on a hard floor or break it with a hammer, collect the water in a bowl and later add it to the coconut milk.

Grate the coconut kernel on a normal scraper or the scythe-like chopper. Allow the grated coconut to stand in two glasses of water for an hour. Strain coconut milk by passing it through a sieve. Pour the coconut milk in a deep pan.

Soak four pieces of wet cocum in a bowl of water for five minutes so that the residue settles at the base of the bowl. Wash the cocum in fresh water and keep aside.

In yet another bowl soak one tablespoon of

uncooked rice for one hour and grind it to a smooth paste or pass through a mixer.

Add salt, chilli, turmeric and cumin to the coconut milk. Then place the vessel on a slow fire, and bring the kadhi to the boil, stirring it continuously. Add the cocum and the rice paste to the kadhi and boil for five more minutes, stirring continuously.

This makes about four bowls of sol kadhi.

Tinned coconut milk can be used if you do not want to make the coconut milk.

Sol kadhi is delicious with plain white rice or even as a hot or cold soup. Bene Israel prefer their sol kadhi with rice and a helping of a spicy kheema, or mincemeat.

Optional: When in season, a few pieces of green mango can be added for a tangy flavour.

If sol kadhi is the queen of curries, then coconut is the king of Jewish cuisine. Every recipe in a Jewish household needs coconut milk as a base. According to the dietary law lamb should not be cooked in its mother's milk. So, instead of dairy products, coconut milk works as a perfect substitute for milk in Bene Israel cuisine.

Influenced by Indian ritual, Jews also believe that coconut is auspicious for new beginnings.

Rachel saw the sea was calm and the fish, which had come as a blessing from the sea, was alive in the bucket. Unable to swim, it was watching her with its beadlike eyes. Rachel carried the bucket to the edge of the water and returned the fish to the sea. She felt relieved.

After Aaron's death, she often made only sol kadhi for herself. It saw her through the day. Rachel liked its colour, cloudy pink, like the sea changing colour under the morning sky. Yet, she never understood why it was known as sol kadhi. It was also known as nariel-chi-kadhi, cocum kadhi or coconut curry. The colour was never golden as the name suggested, but pink because of the cocum. She had noticed that the coconut milk often did not take the exact colour if there was one less piece of cocum.

Rachel often avoided eating alone at the dining table. Instead, she filled her plate with a mound of rice, poured the kadhi in the centre, mixed it well with her fingers and, sitting cross-legged on the veranda, ate in quick morsels, as though she were in a hurry. She usually was, because she then rushed to the synagogue, feeling light-headed and free.

At the synagogue, she stopped and heaved a sigh of relief, away from the house of memories. Covering her head with the end of her sari, she studied the old monument. The palm-studded garden had died. The harsh, dry grass hurt her feet. Creepers from last year's rains had dried in the summer and left their fossil-green designs on the garden wall. The building looked weather-beaten. With every passing year it looked more like a ruin with its chipped Corinthian capitals, moss-covered walls, the arched doorway, the marble plaque with faded Hebrew and Marathi letters.

Inside, the lime had flaked and it was hard to remember the original colour of the walls. Perhaps blue, Rachel thought. The wall, scraped, repainted, faded and flaked, looked like a misty landscape dotted with blue clouds.

The chandeliers, oil lamps and velvet curtains with gold embroidery gave testimony of the synagogue's glorious past, though they were now frayed, charred and greasy.

Rachel had told herself that she would make a new curtain for the synagogue. A white satin curtain embroidered with silver threads, shining like the sea at midday. It would fill her empty hours.

Jews who had left the ancestral village for Israel often sent her cash for the synagogue. Relatives, friends and her own children sent her money more out of a feeling of guilt for having abandoned her. It was enough to repair the synagogue. If she did repair it, was it possible to have a minyan of ten men for the Sabbath service? Without a community, what was the use of a house of prayer? It was just a monument, a relic of the past.

Rachel swept the floor, singing a bhajan to the child Moses floating in a basket on the river Nile. It was a popular Marathi song about the child Krishna. An unknown Jewish poet had changed the name from Krishna to Moses, but the tune was similar to the one sung by Krishna devotees all over Maharashtra. Rachel preferred Marathi bhajans to the complicated Hebrew prayers. She knew their tunes and the occasions for which they were sung.

Rachel washed the floor and wiped the mezuzah with a lace handkerchief she kept in a pocket stitched inside her blouse. Then as a mark of respect she kissed the mezuzah and pulled out the keys of the synagogue from a silver hook tied to her pallav.

Once in a while a villager passing by helped her to open the door and advised her to throw away the old lock and buy a new steel one from the hardware shop in Alibaug. Rachel listened attentively, asking questions as though she would take the next bus to Alibaug and buy one, but never did. She was sure that nobody could ever break into the synagogue. She did not trust new locks: they looked too fragile, not sturdy like the old lock.

Rachel had noticed that sol kadhi gave her extra energy. Ruefully, she remembered that her husband had never relished it. He had an aversion to it. For this very reason, as long as he lived, she rarely made it. If she did make it once in a while, it was for herself, especially when she was feeling cold on a wintry night or when she had a craving for it during one of her pregnancies. As a rule she only made it when Aaron was spending the day in Bombay.

If she ever made it when he was at home, Aaron taunted, pushing away the plate, 'Do you call this food?'

Applying pressure to open the lock, Rachel thought, 'Why are women so sensitive about their husband's preferences? Men never make an effort to adjust to women. They do not bother about their likes or dislikes.'

Since she had married, every single day of her life had revolved around Aaron and the children.

As the key turned in the lock, Rachel decided to make brinjal for dinner. If she did not have mincemeat, she made fried brinjal with sol kadhi and rice. The brinjal came from her vegetable garden. She would pluck two medium-sized brinjals, cut them into roundels and fry them. She liked them crisp with sesame seeds and a dash of red chilli powder. Sol kadhi was the elixir of life. Tonight, after she lit the Sabbath candle, she would not even reheat the coconut curry, as it tasted better cold.

She liked aubergines, similar in colour to the nine-yard sari she had bought on impulse from Laxmi Sari Emporium, a small shop with an assortment of saris, sari-petticoats, Punjabi dresses and blouses. Sometimes they also had the typical Maharashtrian-khand, textiles in bright greens, electric blue, shocking pink, deep maroons and bright yellows. She bought a bottle-green blouse piece to match the sari. On her way back home, she had looked into the plastic bag and smiled. That was not exactly a colour women of her age wore, but there was nothing wrong in wearing a colour of her choice. One day there would be an occasion to wear it.

With one last jerk, the key scraped and as Rachel opened the lock and entered the synagogue a great spiritual aura engulfed her. Whenever she entered the synagogue during the day, she never switched on the lights; instead she opened the windows and let the sunlight stream in.

She swept the marble floor, washed it and mopped it. Then she cleaned the windowpanes with an old, damp newspaper. She liked to give the glass a good shine. Even if she had left it shining like a jewel the week before, the coastal climate was such that in a week the glass became cloudy and dusty. Rachel polished the benches and studied the chandeliers and oil lamps. They needed a good cleaning—she would have to hire someone for that.

There was an old, rickety wooden ladder in the storeroom and sometimes she asked the neighbour's son to climb it and clean the chandeliers, but she was never satisfied. Often she wondered if she could ask him to bring them down, so that she could wash them and wipe them clean with a soft cloth. But the neighbourhood boys were boisterous and she was afraid they would break the ancient lamps. And if the lamps were not secured properly, perhaps they would come crashing down. The thought sent shivers down her spine.

She remembered that an Israeli tourist had gifted one of those metal folding ladders to the synagogue, and she had kept it away in the storeroom. She often brought it out and wondered if she should climb it and clean the chandeliers. But, as usual, she was terrified of falling and breaking a leg and being taken to an unknown hospital in the Promised Land. She folded the ladder and put it away.

Rachel made a mental note to ask Aviv to send her some of those fancy Israeli sprays to give that extra sparkle to glass. The last time Aviv had left a spray to clean windows, she had used it for three years and the glass shone like crystal.

Rachel took a deep breath as she remembered its lavender fragrance. It was just like the aftershave her husband once sprayed on himself before posing for a photograph in the drawing room under the clock. She did not understand his logic of wearing perfume just for a photograph.

In the photograph, Aaron was wearing his deep-brown three-piece suit with a mauve tie, dotted with sprigs of lavender. She kept it in one of her many trunks. The silk of the tie was frayed, with a big, vertical tear in the centre. But, whenever she opened this particular trunk, the strong fragrance of lavender hit her. Lavender meant desire and love.

There was also another memory connected with lavender. It was that of a strange flower she had seen in one of those farmhouses near Alibaug. These flowers were harvested here and were supposed to be very expensive. They grew like creepers on trees and had huge, speckled petals like wings of butterflies.

The Alibaug climate was supposed to be just right to grow them. Rachel had heard that the owners of these gardens were buying up all the land around the synagogue. She shivered in the rain and covered herself with the end of her sari. An estate agent had recently come to see her land and the areas around Danda. She dreaded the day they would prey upon the land of the Lord. To distract herself, she threw one last look at the synagogue and was pleased that it looked neat, clean and holy. She locked it with a heavy heart, as there was nobody there to light the Sabbath candle, neither rabbi, cantor nor Aaron.

The minyan of ten men was a distant dream. She kissed the mezuzah and sat on the veranda, watching the late afternoon light, her heart filling with a strange sadness. She dusted it off like a speck of sand from her sari and rushed home to cook the brinjals before the Sabbath set upon the sea.

Rachel told herself she would light a candle, fill the Kiddush cup with grape sherbet, break the Sabbath bhakhri in two, touch it with salt and pray for the synagogue.

MUTTON CURRY
WITH TAMARIND

Ingredients: mutton, oil, onions, potatoes, garlic, ginger, turmeric, red chilli, coriander, cumin, cinnamon, cloves, tamarind, coconut milk, sugar, salt

Method: You need half a kilogram of meat of goat or lamb: cleaned, washed and cubed.

The meat can be pressure cooked in advance and added to the masala.

Heat oil in a casserole; brown two sliced onions; add a tablespoon ginger–garlic paste, half a teaspoon each of powdered red chilli, coriander and cumin, cinnamon and cloves, turmeric and salt; stir. Add a cup of mutton stock or a glass of water and cook till masala absorbs oil. Add the meat; stir well. Cook in two glasses of water or stock, adding potatoes at the end. When done, lower flame and slowly mix two tablespoons tamarind pulp with half teaspoon sugar; cook for five more minutes, adding a cup coconut milk till the gravy thickens. Serve hot with rice, puris or chapattis.

Tamarind is a natural cleanser, be it of brass or bowels. It is used for shining metal vessels like brass and copper.

Rachel often sat under the tamarind tree in the courtyard of the synagogue, breathing deep of the fragrance of its fresh, young leaves and savouring the sweet and sour memories of the first year of her marriage. It brought a smile to her wrinkled cheeks.

This particular tamarind tree was ancient. According to myth, it was the abode of ghosts. The land was fertile and the tamarind abundant. Although the tree was very close to the house, on dark nights she made a detour of the tree to avoid its shadow. She had been told that on dark, moonless nights, ghosts roosted there.

It had a huge hollow in its trunk and once, while returning from Alibaug in the family bullock cart, Rachel got the distinct feeling that somebody was watching her from inside the tree. She was sure the ghosts were casting a spell on her, but was relieved to hear the familiar flutter of the barn owl's wings. The tree's shadow had fallen over the synagogue and she had felt she was in the protective presence of her ancestors. Since then the tamarind had become her guardian angel.

The tamarind was again heavy with fruit and she spent her afternoons there, chasing away the children of the neighbourhood. They climbed the tree to pluck its fruit or threw stones to knock the ripe pods to the ground. She had already asked the contractor to harvest the crop. With the extra cash she would get the broken windows of the synagogue repaired and even ask the carpenter to apply a layer of varnish on the benches.

Rachel sat on the veranda, still like a statue, watching the tree and listening to the birds. She had grown accustomed to Danda, its sounds and its silence. She had woken up early and, after a leisurely bath, had seen one of the neighbours pass by in his bullock cart. She had called out to him and asked if he would please drop her at the Alibaug market. Having bought the groceries, she went to the Alibaug synagogue to buy kosher meat for herself.

Hazzan Hassaji Daniyal, the old cantor of the synagogue, still continued to work as a butcher for the community. 'Look how thin you have become,' he said. 'A bag of bones! Not eating properly, are you?'

Rachel smiled. 'How much do you think one person needs to eat? I am strong like a horse and all these delicacies like mutton and fish are no fun to eat when you are alone.'

'Eat for yourself,' the cantor advised Rachel as she took an autorickshaw back to Danda.

She returned feeling hungry and mixed some leftover rice in a bowl of curd and ate it standing next to the fridge. Rachel liked her curries with chapattis or rice. But feeling too lazy to cook one single chapatti for herself, she had stopped at Alibaug's Rustom Bakery to pick up a loaf of bread.

Rachel browned the onions, strained the tamarind pulp and peeled the potatoes to thicken the gravy—the tamarind would lend a subtle sour–sweet flavour to the meat. She squeezed the fresh fruit of tamarind in her palm, soft and full of brown liquid; the black seeds, like pebbles of granite, slipped from her fingers and fell into the pan.

In her younger days, Rachel could eat raw tamarind, but since she had lost some of her teeth, she could no longer eat anything sour. Yet, she never missed a chance of adding tamarind to her dal, curries or chutneys, if the recipe demanded it.

With a smile, Rachel remembered the day she had climbed the tamarind tree after her marriage. Looking up at the tree in the courtyard, Rachel had assumed it was a hundred feet tall. She particularly liked its small-leafed foliage, the bright-pink flowers, the young fruit, flat, green, soft and crisp, and the sour–sweet fragrance which pervaded the house.

Tamarind was a major source of income for the family. They had an abundant crop of coconut, areca nut and tamarind. Labourers collected the fruit, sorted it, cleaned it and packed it in baskets for the market, and the women of the house stocked a year's supply in ceramic jars.

Ever since Rachel had come to the house as a young bride, the tamarind tree had attracted her. Often, when she was alone in the house, she stood on the veranda and studied it, but had kept away from it, as she had been taught that a married woman was not supposed to climb trees or jump around like a virgin monkey.

She felt like Eve watching the forbidden fruit. The tree looked bewitching; it seemed to call out to her to explore its mystery.

Once, when nobody was at home, Rachel could resist no more.

Except Aaron, the rest of the family had gone to Bombay for a funeral. Her mother-in-law had left specific instructions with Rachel to finish the housework and prepare the evening meal.

Aaron had left early for Alibaug to meet a coconut contractor. Feeling free and liberated for a day, Rachel tied her sari over her thighs and climbed the tree. She sat there like a langur, breathing deep into its fragrance, and looked longingly at the ripe fruit, full of seed and crusty brown.

Rachel climbed higher up and sat there, swinging her legs, enjoying the freedom she had lost when she married Aaron. The set of rules and regulations for new brides suffocated her and she never had the courage to tell anybody that she was bored and needed to run wild in the fields.

Sitting on a branch, Rachel had her fill of the tamarind till it made her teeth tingle. When the sweet–sour flavour had seeped into her being, she picked a ripe fruit and tied it into the end of her sari for later. Then she started descending, but realized that she could not climb down without help. She prayed for help. She trembled with fear that she would be caught red-handed. Perhaps her mother-in-law would scold her and punish her for such childish behaviour, ashamed that a daughter-in-law of the house had the audacity to climb a tree and expose the family to unnecessary shame. If her mother-in-law ever saw her sitting there, she would ask her to jump down and die.

From her vantage point, Rachel saw that the sun was about to set on the Arabian Sea and she was afraid that her mother-in-law and the ghosts would both appear together. She panicked, as she didn't know how to get down, except to jump and break her leg. She was cold and afraid as she watched the bats flying towards her with outstretched wings, merging in the darkness of the foliage, then hanging upside down and screeching like newborn babies. And then a cloud of mosquitoes descended. She found it hard to ward them off, cover herself with the sari and keep her balance.

It was then that she heard the bells of the family bullock cart approaching the house. It was music to her ears. With a thumping heart, Rachel watched the bullock cart stop at the gate of the house. She saw Aaron unyoking the bullocks, calling out to her, to give him a hand with the bags of groceries.

He seemed surprised that Rachel had not rushed out of the house to greet him. He had returned early to surprise her. But the doors of the house stood wide open and there was nobody inside. It was dark and he was annoyed that Rachel had not even bothered to light the hurricane lamps. Where was she?

Somebody, seeing her alone in the house, he was sure, had kidnapped her. Had he lost her, just when he was falling in love with her? He had not found her attractive when she was a gangly girl of nine or ten and he had tried to argue with his mother, 'I don't want to get married to Rachel. We have shared the same cradle and played the same games. She is too familiar. I have known her since she was a baby. Besides that, she is much too skinny for my liking.'

His mother had answered, 'Just wait and see how she fills up after marriage. Girls like Rachel take time to blossom.'

But Aaron had grumbled, 'Am I supposed to wait till she fills up?'

His mother had laughed it off. 'Just wait and see,' she said.

Aaron had slowly come to accept his skinny but cheerful wife.

He liked her smile; it filled her face like a sunflower. He enjoyed her playfulness. It did not matter that her body never filled up. She remained as thin as a reed. And slowly he came to appreciate her.

Aaron ran around the house looking for her, cursing himself for leaving her alone in the house. Rachel wanted to call out to him, but did not say anything, afraid that he would scold her for climbing trees.

She sat frozen on the branch, as she saw Aaron run from room to room, till he stood panting in the courtyard, trying to light a lantern with shaky hands. Then she saw him peeping into the well and almost gave herself away with her giggles.

The well stood next to the house. For the women, the platform next to the well was the centre of all activities. Their lives revolved around the well. All morning, they filled drinking water in pots, troughs and cauldrons. Another container stood in the corner of the veranda for collecting rainwater. It was used for washing hands and feet before entering the house. Sometimes the men bathed there, while the women carried bucketsful into the bath-place behind the house, made with dry palm leaves.

Some pots of water were also kept in the rajodarshan room, a separate room, where women were isolated during their menstrual cycle and during childbirth.

Aaron was looking into the well. She had often told him that while drawing water she was afraid of falling into the well. Being frail and thin, she had to apply all her strength on the pulley to get the brass pots out of the well. She feared that the pots would pull her back into the well, so with feet firmly planted on the platform she would keep pulling till the pot reached the edge and she could grab its rim with relief.

Aaron was sure she had fallen into the well and, peeping into the darkness, he called out to Rachel. She heard the eerie echo of her name emerging from the well. That is when Rachel laughed and heard another echo, 'Rachel where are you?'

'Here.'

Aaron looked up confused. He could not see her in the dark shadows of the tree, not expecting her to be there.

'Where are you?'

Again, he heard her voice, but did not see her. 'Promise you will not get angry.'

'I promise.' His voice trembled.

'Look up here, in the tamarind tree,' she said. 'I am on this branch and cannot climb down without your help.'

It was getting dark and Aaron saw her shadow move like a ghost in the tamarind tree. Quickly, he climbed up the tree and holding her hand helped her down.

He stopped for a second at the fork of the tree, holding her in his arms, caressing her deep-brown skin, velvety soft like the ripe fruit of the tamarind. They clung to each other, kissing passionately. Aaron smiled when he felt her lips moving under his: swollen, purple and sour.

He asked her to stay where she was, because he was sure if she jumped down her legs would snap like twigs. He climbed down and asked her to jump into his arms. Rachel closed her eyes and, with her heart beating wildly, fell into his arms. Aaron carried her into the house and they made love like never before.

When they woke up, Rachel realized that the tamarind was still tied in a knot at the end of her sari and she was hungry. Aaron was watching her and pulled her back into his arms. She giggled and, caressing his stomach, asked if he was hungry.

Rachel's mother-in-law had boiled the mutton and left it standing in a bowl of water, covered and hanging in a wire container fixed to the ceiling of the kitchen. Rachel thanked the lord that neither cat nor crow had touched the meat, for then she would have had to make bombil, Bombay duck, dried and stored in containers on the kitchen rack. But how would she have accounted for the disappearance of the mutton?

She did not want her mother-in-law to taunt her that she was an inefficient daughter-in-law, no good for her precious son, Aaron. Rachel looked at the pan of meat and did not know what to do with it. Young that she was, she had not yet taken full charge of the kitchen and was not ready to take serious decisions about food. So far, she had only been helper to both mother and mother-in-law.

From the kitchen doorway, she saw Aaron washing at the well and called out to him, 'Shall I make a simple curry or something special?'

Aaron came to the kitchen door, smiled and said, 'With tamarind?'

PEETHAL

Ingredients: gram flour, water, oil, onion, garlic, turmeric powder, cumin powder, mustard seeds, coriander leaves, salt to taste

Method: Take a cup of gram flour in a bowl, slowly blend in a tablespoon of oil, half a teaspoon each of powdered cumin, turmeric, salt and a cup of water, mixing it with the flour, a little at a time, to make a thick batter with a creamy consistency.

Heat one tablespoon oil in a pan, temper a few mustard seeds, brown one chopped onion with half a teaspoon garlic paste, slowly fold in the batter, stirring continuously till the batter thickens and leaves the pan. Garnish with fresh coriander leaves.

Peethal, also known as pithle or zunka, is made in liquid form or dry, according to personal preferences in a family. Dry peethal can be also cut into bite-size pieces.

When made dry and thicker in consistency, peethal is known as zunka and often served with bajra bhakhras or chapattis.

Optional: Roast gram flour before mixing the gram flour batter for peethal.

❧

Dal–rice is the staple diet of most Indians, including Bene Israel Jews. It is made almost every day in Indian homes.

There are many varieties of lentils like toovar, moong and chana.

Chana dal and doodhi, or marrow, is often made as the main meal and served with rice.

Chana atta or gram flour is used to make peethal.

Chana is delicious when eaten green, raw, roasted, cooked, boiled, made into dal or even as a batter to fry bhajjis or vegetable fritters.

A favourite Indian pastime is to munch chana, roasted or deep fried. Dal dishes offer many possibilities and variations.

Gram flour is also used to make a home-made face mask with milk, turmeric, rose water and powdered almonds. It cleanses and whitens the skin and lends a glow to the face.

When Rachel's sons, Aviv and Jacob, came to Danda with their families, the house would resound with laughter. Sometimes, distant relatives from Israel, Bombay, Pune or Ahmedabad, like Malkha and Esther, came to see Rachel.

With family around her, Rachel enjoyed cooking. After all, she had grown up in a big family, married into a bigger family and raised a fairly large family herself. When her guests left, Rachel felt sad and lonely and spent a listless week feeling out of sorts, till she got back to her day-to-day rhythm around the synagogue. It was one of those normal sort of days, when Rachel was not expecting any guests. She was sitting in her chair on the veranda and brushing Brownie when an autorickshaw stopped at her gate and she saw Mordecai standing at her door. He was one of the members of the synagogue committee. Rachel knew him well as he was one of Aaron's childhood friends.

He often came to meet her, as she was the unofficial caretaker of the synagogue. Her house, being closest to the synagogue, was the ideal place to keep the keys. He had noticed that she kept the synagogue clean, as though she was preparing for the arrival of a congregation.

Mordecai was in his seventies and walked with a stoop, his hands folded behind his back. He had a square jaw and innumerable warts on his face. He lived in Bombay and always wore loose white trousers, white bush shirts and black sandals.

Whenever Mordecai visited her, Rachel never failed to notice his hooked toenails. Although he was very polite and respectful, she disliked him, though she could never say what it was about him that made her feel that he was evil. But when she spoke to him, she made sure that her expression was polite. Not being a very sensitive man, he never noticed the slight change of expression on her face.

On this particular visit, Mordecai was carrying a packet in his hand. It looked like a gift. Rachel was suspicious about him, knowing that he always had something up his sleeve. She especially disliked his small, shifty eyes. She noticed that the cylindrical plastic box he was carrying had a flower inside.

She was annoyed. It had the colour and fragrance of lavender, the type she always associated with her husband. It reminded her of his aftershave lotion and Rachel felt that Mordecai had invaded the privacy of her memories.

She threw an annoyed look at the flower asking, 'Were you buying flowers in Alibaug? I have heard they grow these very English flowers there. How come you are interested in them?' She narrowed her eyes and gave him a cynical smile.

Mordecai was not one to be defeated by a woman. Especially Rachel. He had known her for too many years and was rather wary of her sharp tongue. He left the flower with its mauve and red speckled petals on the parapet saying, 'It is a gift from Mr Chinoy. He has a farm in Alibaug.'

'A what?' asked Rachel.

'A farm where he grows exotic flowers like orchids.'

'Is that the name of this flower?'

'Yes. Aren't they beautiful?'

'This one looks sort of fancy.'

'Do you like it?'

'I have never seen a flower like this before, so I cannot give you an opinion. I am not even sure if I can call it a flower.'

'Well, these are special flowers and have a big market. They say the Alibaug air is very good for flowers.'

Rachel stared at the flower. 'So, how will it affect our lives?'

Mordecai saw that Rachel was not impressed; she had been watching the orchid from a distance as though it was a demon.

Mordecai smiled. 'The flower is a gift for you from Mr Chinoy.'

'Ah!' said Rachel. 'What do you think I am going to do with a flower like this?' She doubled up with laughter. 'At my age, you do not expect me to stick it in my hair like a sixteen-year-old.'

Then, throwing him a suspicious glance, Rachel asked, 'I know you have not come here to discuss flowers, so tell me what is on your mind.'

Rachel sat regally on her chair, head covered with her pallav, legs crossed, hands clasped in her lap.

Mordecai spoke in an even tone. 'Mr Chinoy has offered a very good price for the land around the synagogue. He is going to pay us well. So we may accept his offer and sell this land to him.'

With a look of distaste, Rachel asked him, 'And what happens to the synagogue?'

'That,' he said with a deadpan face, 'will be Mr Chinoy's property. He will perhaps make it into a greenhouse or he could even level it down. After all, it is almost a ruin and do you think it will ever be of any use to us? Look, most Jews have left for Israel.'

Rachel threw him a suspicious glance. 'This Mr Chinoy of yours, has he seen the land?'

'Yes. While he was driving past, he just had a look at it. For a man of his experience, one glance is good enough. He knows what he wants. And, now that his business is growing, he would like to expand it around here. You see, he is a very busy man, but one of these days he will come to meet you. In fact, I told him about you. He is also interested in your place as it faces the sea. I think he is planning to make a health resort along the seashore. Actually he could employ you and you could live an easy life.'

'Employ?' she asked, her temper rising. 'At my age? Are you suggesting that I work as a servant for Mr Chinoy? My husband and children have seen to it that I live a comfortable life. Does he think I am the caretaker of the synagogue just because I am poor and need the money? Has anybody ever paid me a salary? Or have I ever asked the trustees for money? Do you think I am employed at the synagogue and that I need a job? All these years, I have been a servant of the Lord, not of your synagogue committee. How dare you suggest anything like this or assume that I want to sell my land!' She stood up angrily, picked up the tea cups and said, 'I have no intention of selling my house.'

'Mr Chinoy is a very good man. He would not even harm an ant. Even if he buys your house, he will give you another flat in Alibaug. It will be a very good deal.'

Rachel shot back, 'Why are you discussing my house without my permission?'

Mordecai explained hurriedly, 'I am just trying to help.'

'No need,' she said and went into the kitchen and whiled away some time washing the cups, hoping Mordecai would eventually leave. She peeped out of the window and saw he was sitting there, hands resting on his knees.

Rachel returned and asked, 'Now what next?'

Mordecai gave her a sideways look and understood that convincing Rachel was not going to be an easy matter. He wondered how Aaron had spent a lifetime with this stubborn little woman. He had known Aaron since they were boys, and had always known Rachel to be his obedient wife. Little had he realized that Rachel was a self-willed, strong woman and that the synagogue had become the mission of her life.

It was already lunchtime, the sea was a shimmering sheet of silver, but Rachel was not thinking about food. Normally she offered him lunch of vades, puris, bhajis, batata-poha or whatever she had in the house, but today she did not say anything. Mordecai sensed her resentment, but he was hungry. So he asked her if there was some place where he could get a thali. He had left Bombay early and it would be hours before he got back.

Rachel almost felt like telling him to take an autorickshaw to Murud, where he would get a thali at a roadside restaurant. But she could not be so rude. Instead, she said, 'I am sorry, I should have offered you lunch. But you gave me such a shock when you spoke about selling the synagogue that I wasn't even thinking about food.'

'Really Rachelbai, you must not be so sentimental about such matters. Do you think the synagogue will ever be of any use to anybody? It is a ruin,' he said with a tone of finality.

Rachel ignored his words and changed the subject. 'Since my husband died, I rarely cook lunch. I start thinking about food in the evening. Let me see what I have in the kitchen. I have some chapattis. Or perhaps I can make some peethal for you.'

Mordecai smiled. 'I often remember those good old days when Aaron used to insist that I eat lunch before leaving for Bombay. I remember, you made the best peethal I ever had, just like my mother's. But my wife refuses to make it for me, saying it gives me acidity. Actually, she is a Bombay girl, so she thinks peethal is food for farmers.'

A compliment always worked well with Rachel. At last she smiled. 'Of course, it is food for villagers. Let me see if I have any flour in the house.'

Rachel opened the bottle of gram flour and saw that she had just enough for the peethal. She chopped an onion, peeled the garlic and made the batter. As she sprinkled turmeric and stirred it in, the golden-yellow colour of the batter reminded her of fresh mustard fields. They were part of her childhood. When she was a child, her mother was always worried that she was darker than the other children.

Rachel was then not yet thirteen. She was tall, thin, knock-kneed and scraggly and looked like a girl of nine. When she reached puberty, Rachel felt she had breasts under her blouse, small and taut like raw green mangoes. When the first menstrual blood had trickled down her thighs, her mother had helped her wear a cloth and proclaimed in a curt, hard voice, 'Now you are a woman and ripe enough to have a baby.'

Her mother's serious expression had frightened Rachel. That was one of the main reasons that Rachel had not told her mother that curly hair had appeared between her legs, and her body had a delicious smell. Rachel had assumed it was all because of the blood.

Whenever Rachel tried to broach the topic about her body, her mother's face hardened with distaste. Rachel avoided asking her mother the questions that crowded her mind. Since she had felt the wetness of her own blood between her thighs, there was a certain distance between them. Instinctively she sensed that the subject was taboo.

Once she had been taught to wear the cloth, no more discussion was encouraged and she was expected to work out her problems with sisters, girlfriends or cousins.

Rachel remembered that when her wedding date had been fixed she was depressed. Every morning, she looked into the mirror and felt she was much too dark to be a bride. Brides were supposed to be fair and beautiful. Her mother would look at her disapprovingly and say, 'You must do something about your skin.'

Rachel would burst into tears and her mother would scrub her face with a good soap, rub the skin with a towel till it hurt and apply a paste of gram flour mixed with fresh milk and cream. Perhaps one day she would become fairer. Yet, there was no denying that on her wedding day Rachel looked beautiful.

Much later, Rachel had tried the same remedy on Zephra. Rachel's mother had taught her to make a batter of gram flour, turmeric, cream, rose water and crushed almonds, which she applied on Zephra's face and neck to lighten her skin. Far away in Israel, Zephra cherished those distant, tender moments. Rachel ached for her daughter whenever she made a batter of gram flour.

This was one reason she had become an expert at mixing peethal to its right consistency. Rachel's mother had taught her early in life that when there was nothing else in the house peethal was easy to prepare. It was simple, quick, easy, nourishing and heavy, and stayed in the stomach for a long time. But it had a tendency to give gas, so it was necessary to take long walks after eating peethal.

Her mother had also taught her the mantra: 'When chana atta is used to clear the skin, never allow it to dry so much that it pulls at the skin and hurts. When it dries, remove it with a sponge or wash it under the tap while it is still soft. Then study your face. If not fair, it will definitely soften your skin like a rose petal and your husband will love you.'

For years, Rachel had applied gram flour to her face before her bath, wondering if there was a certain type of chana that would transform her colour from black to white.

Rachel had fond memories of the night before her marriage. Her cousins and girlfriends had surrounded her for the mehndi ceremony, wrapping her in a half sari from bosom to thigh and applying a paste of freshly ground turmeric to her body.

With their ribald jokes Rachel had glowed and her mother had been pleased. Sitting on the wooden stool, Rachel had caught the look of appreciation in her mother's eyes and asked, 'Is this the magic of chana?'

Her mother had taken a handful of the paste and applied it to her forehead, saying, 'It is the spice of life.'

Rachel stirred the peethal with a vengeance and offered Mordecai a plate of peethal and chapattis, hoping that, by the time he reached Bombay, he would get an attack of acidity and his wife would scold him for eating something as ordinary as peethal.

But before that she would remind him to take back his precious flower to Bombay. She did not want it in her house.

CHICKEN KESARI

Ingredients: chicken, oil, onions, ginger, garlic, turmeric powder, red chillies, cloves, peppercorns, cardamom, cinnamon, tomatoes, coconut, salt to taste, saffron

Method: Cut one chicken into ten pieces. Wash, salt and keep aside. Extract one glass of milk from half a coconut with fleshy kernel. Roast a tablespoon of grated coconut on a griddle till golden brown; pass through a mixer and keep aside.

Soak four to five threads of saffron in a bowl of warm water and let it stand till water changes colour to orange.

Heat two tablespoons oil in a karhai; temper with two cloves, a stick cinnamon and two cardamoms. Brown one big onion chopped fine. Add a teaspoon ginger–garlic paste, half a teaspoon red chilli powder, a pinch turmeric with two finely chopped tomatoes, roasted paste of coconut and allow to cook on a slow

fire till masala absorbs oil. Mix chicken pieces with
the masala; add a glass of water and cook till tender;
add coconut milk and saffron water. Garnish with
coriander leaves and cover with a tight lid. Cook for
five more minutes and remove from fire. Keep covered
to retain the flavour of saffron and open lid before
serving hot with rice.

Variation: Use pressure-cooked mutton for the
same recipe.

❧

*Saffron—kesar—is a name given to the stamens of a mauve crocus
flower, which grows in Kashmir. The stamen has three bright-
saffron-coloured threads, which are handpicked. It takes many
crocus flowers to get a small quantity of saffron. Normally it is
kept in a coin-sized box.*

*Kesar looks like strings of dry grass. It yields a wonderful
saffron colour when soaked in warm water. A few strings of
saffron can lend a heady aroma and rich colour to rice, curries or
desserts.*

No Indian kitchen is complete without saffron.

Rachel was restless. She made innumerable rounds between
the house and the synagogue and did not know what to do.
She wanted the synagogue to come alive with people and
celebrations like the good old days. She reasoned with herself
that she did not own the synagogue. It belonged to the community.
But nobody ever came to the synagogue any more. The few Bene
Israel living on the Konkan coast preferred to visit one of the
bigger synagogues at Thane, Alibaug, Pen or Panvel. Nobody
ever came to Danda.

Most synagogues on the Konkan coast were locked and
abandoned. Their respective committees held innumerable

discussions about their fate, yet most synagogues were slowly turning into ruins. Rachel often heard about thefts of chandeliers, light bulbs or even benches and was relieved that so far there had been no theft from her synagogue.

'My synagogue?' Rachel asked herself. 'Now, whoever said it was *my* synagogue? Can it be mine just because I clean it, wash it, polish the benches and look after it as though it is my house? I must never forget that it is the house of God, a synagogue, which is in the custody of a committee, a committee of men. After all, I am a woman,' she reasoned. 'There are so many laws for women. For example, can I ever climb the teva and clean it?' she muttered.

'No,' she answered herself, 'a woman is unclean because of her menstrual blood.' Early in her life she had been taught that the teva was the domain of men. A woman cannot step on it without the permission of men. A woman's feet touches the teva only if ritual demands it, like a marriage or a blessing, or her own wedding when she stands on the teva with her groom. Sometimes, on the Sabbath or festivals, some women, when clean, bowed at the chair of the Prophet Elijah or climbed the platform of the Ark to touch the curtain, asking for health and happiness for their family, but they never climbed the teva. Whenever Rachel looked at the teva, she cringed at the thought that she was a woman. She had always kept away from the teva.

But she had noticed it was dirty. The wood had lost its sheen and the star-spangled design of the textile was covered with dust. The holy books had also collected layers of dust. The velvet on the chairs had lost their original colour, the lamps on the four posts of the teva were full of dead insects and the iron grill had a layer of grime.

For years, Rachel had seen to it that the rest of the synagogue was neat and clean, but the teva stood in a column of dust, untouched, unattended. She was sure that the silver Kiddush cup must have rusted with the sediment of wine from the last Sabbath. Now how many years ago was that? Every time Rachel entered the synagogue, the dusty teva hurt like a grain of sand in her eye. But everything had changed for Rachel when an American rabbi came to the synagogue a few years ago. Rachel tried hard to recall his name, but could not. She only remembered that his name began with something like a 'Na' and ended with a 'son'.

The synagogue committee was escorting him on his tour of the synagogues on the Konkan coast. Mordecai had informed her in advance. Rachel had washed and cleaned the synagogue and employed labourers to clean the courtyard. She had even carried some flower pots from her house and arranged them on the veranda and tied a string of mango leaves on the dilapidated archway.

The rabbi appreciated her efforts, but was shocked to see that the teva had not been cleaned in years. The men rushed to wipe the tables, raising a cloud of dust. They explained apologetically that Rachel was a woman and could not possibly touch the teva. They would call hazzan Hassaji Daniyal from Alibaug and ask him to clean it regularly. The rabbi turned red, saying, 'A woman like Rachel cannot possibly be impure. Look at her dedication to the synagogue. Anyway, do you really care for it? I do not think you will ever hold a Sabbath service here again. Does it matter who cleans it—man or woman? Honestly, this is ridiculous.'

Everybody, including Rachel, understood the meaning of his words. He had said in no uncertain terms that Rachel was past the menopausal age and there was no harm if she touched the teva. And even if she was menstruating, it did not matter, as she was dedicated to the synagogue. For Rachel, this was the moment of freedom from the confines of age-old traditions and taboos.

Rachel stood at the synagogue door, watching the entourage leave with the rabbi. As he was getting into the car, rabbi Nahson suddenly stopped, walked back to where Rachel was standing and reached out his hand, thanking her profusely. She stood dumbstruck, not knowing what to do. Embarrassed, she looked at her feet and hesitantly offered him her hand. He shook hands with her and left with a look of admiration. It was then that the committee followed his example and returned to thank her.

The president of the committee said, 'Sister Rachel, from now on you can touch the teva.'

Much later, Hassaji Daniyal, the old cantor, told Rachel that the rabbi had reprimanded the committee, saying, 'You are lucky to have Rachel Dandekar, a holy lady. She looks after the synagogue so well. It is hard to believe that you do not hold services there.'

When Rachel was younger, her life revolved around her home and the synagogue. There were a hundred and one reasons to go to the synagogue, the weekly Sabbath services, an Eliyahu Hannabi, a festival, a wedding, circumcision of a male child or a bar mitzvah.

As a child, Rachel remembered, a visit to the synagogue meant having a good bath and wearing clean, new clothes. The girls wore new blouses with puffed sleeves over bright long skirts. The older women oiled their hair, braided the plaits with tassels and tied a string of flowers with a small handkerchief pinned at the back of their head. They wore their best saris and gold jewellery. Once in a while the younger girls were allowed to wear a new pair of earrings, a nose ring, new glass bangles and anklets. The boys wore embroidered skullcaps and new shirts over loose pants.

After prayers, the children were allowed to play in the courtyard. And, if they played hide-and-seek around the teva, nobody stopped them, but the girls knew that they were not to climb the teva. It was an unbroken rule.

Rachel stood at the door, watching the teva in amazement. All alone in the silent synagogue, she felt strangely elated. The dusty teva transformed into the ethereal Mount Sion. It was shining with a brilliance she had never seen before. It was no longer just a rectangular arrangement of tables on a raised marble platform facing Jerusalem, but a mountain that proclaimed the glory of the Lord. She felt she was in the presence of something bigger and more beautiful than human existence.

Hesitant, Rachel walked towards the teva. The rabbi had given her a gift of the gods. But an unknown hand seemed to stop her; the years of training stood between Rachel and the teva. She moved backwards towards the door, feeling strangely vulnerable.

Standing near the first step of the teva, her first instinct was to run away from the house of God as she told herself, 'These foreigners don't understand anything. I suppose the president did not mean anything. He got carried away by the rabbi's sentiment.'

Rachel started trembling. Then, like one in a dream, she started walking towards the teva again. There was an aura around it, which seemed to beckon her. Each step was like a century. Her feet felt leaden as she moved towards the teva. With each step, the tears streamed down her cheeks. As soon as she stepped on the teva, her body became as light as a feather. Rachel stopped breathing. She felt she had been running for years and had finally reached her destination. The touch of the marble was cool and comforting. Rachel cried till she was spent of all emotion.

Standing still on the platform of the teva, Rachel touched her head to the Torah, asking forgiveness of the Lord for going against the law. She collected the books, the Sabbath plate, the Kiddush cup and a small silver frame of the Ten Commandments in Hebrew and respectfully left them on the chair of the Prophet Elijah.

Returning to the teva, she removed the ancient tablecloth. She then pulled out the carpet from under the platform, dragged it to the veranda and dusted it. The dust was billowing around her like a cloud. She left it to sun and returned to wipe the tables and wash the platform with a bucket of water. She rubbed the tables and floors till her hands ached and the marble shone like ivory. Rachel was pleased with her handiwork, but did not want to cover the tables again with the same dusty cloth.

She went to the storeroom where pots and pans for all rituals were kept. While rummaging in the cupboards, she had once found old bed sheets and carpets, folded and kept between layers of thin muslin and tobacco leaves. There was a strong, musty smell of mothballs, but everything inside the cupboard was clean as though somebody had just put away the laundry. With utmost care, Rachel lifted the fragile layers and saw that there was a blue bed sheet with a design of stars and a clean red carpet, tattered at the edges but otherwise in a good condition. Rachel carried these back to the teva.

She spread out the cloth on the table and the carpet on the floor. After years, the teva looked clean and beautiful. She then washed the Sabbath tray, the wineglass and the plate of salt before she arranged them back on the table.

With the end of her sari, Rachel wiped the books and the frame of the Ten Commandments. She touched them to her head before laying them back where they had stood for years.

Everything looked perfect, yet something was amiss. There was no light. A candle would shed light in the house of God.

Rachel hesitated, unsure whether she was allowed to light a lamp or not. Then she told herself that she would listen to her heart. She took a clay lamp from the storeroom, poured some oil from a bottle she kept hidden behind the chair of Eliyahu Hannabi and lit the lamp, placing it at the base of the steps because she did not want to take any chances with the law.

The lamp was small, yet the entire synagogue glowed with an aura Rachel had not seen in years. With the mere act of lighting a lamp, she experienced a sense of accomplishment. For the first time in years, there was light in the synagogue.

It was her private moment of victory, when she felt she was in perfect communion with the Lord, so she waited for the lamp to burn out. Then she locked the door and saw that the evening sun had set the sky ablaze with a saffron tinge.

Slowly, Rachel walked back to the house. The colours of the sky reflected in the soft waves of the sea and she wanted to rejoice. She would celebrate this special gift from the rabbi by making an elaborate dinner for herself. It would have the colour of the evening sky. It was good that she had bought some chicken that morning. She would cook it in saffron.

For Rachel, her box of saffron was as precious as her gold.

She kept it hidden in a small box, tightly packed, and used it sparingly for festive dinners. Saffron, she told herself, would be the symbol of her freedom.

Before she started preparations for dinner, Rachel ran the geyser and had a bath. She wanted to wash off the layers of dust from her body and mind. Then she pulled out a freshly washed white sari dotted with yellow flowers. To match her mood, Rachel applied a drop of eau de cologne on her temples and dabbed some powder on her face. Feeling fresh and happy, Rachel started looking for her box of saffron.

Normally Rachel kept all her expensive spices in the meat safe. But she did not keep the saffron with the bottles of masalas as the strong flavour of other spices would overpower its subtle floral fragrance.

Rachel looked high and low in the meat safe, but could not find the box of saffron. She had a vague memory that she had kept it in a small plastic box. She rummaged through all the kitchen shelves but did not find it. She was disheartened, as she had decided to make chicken kesari after years. She remembered that she had last made it when her first grandchild was born in Israel.

She remembered that day clearly. There was a long-distance call from her son Aviv. Excited, he had told her that she had just become a grandmother. From across the seven seas she could hear the echo of her own voice as she wept and congratulated her son. She could hear the echo of her own tear-filled voice as she asked, 'Is it a son or a daughter?'

'Daughter,' her son had said.

As soon as she had put the receiver back on the cradle, Rachel had slumped on the floor, crying. What misfortune, she cursed herself, that her first grandchild was born and she was sitting all alone in Danda, far away from the family. Her family was to multiply in the Promised Land.

Rachel had cried so much that her neighbour Kirtibai had rushed to comfort her. She did not know what had made Rachel cry. When she noticed the receiver was not placed properly, she assumed Rachel had received some bad news from Israel.

Placing the receiver back on the cradle, she put her arm around Rachel's shoulders, wiped her tears and asked, 'Tell me, what is the matter?'

Rachel sobbed, 'I just became a grandmother and I cannot even hold the little one in my arms.'

Kirtibai started laughing as though it was the funniest thing on earth and, offering her a glass of water, said, 'Arre, the way you were crying, I thought you had received some bad news from Israel.'

Rachel placed a finger on Kirtibai's lips and said, 'No, no, the birth of a baby is good news.'

Kirtibai smiled. 'Rachelbai, we must celebrate the arrival of the little one with pedas, nako?' She was laughing.

Kirtibai called out to the women of the neighbourhood, and sent one of them to buy the sweets. When the pedas arrived, Kirtibai distributed the sweets, singing a kirtan to the baby Krishna.

Rachel was beaming as she wondered what the baby looked like. Perhaps just like Krishna, plump and all smiles. She wondered if the child was as dark as Krishna.

The younger women of the neighbourhood were all over the house; some were on the swing and others had climbed the tamarind tree. The house resounded with laughter, the way it used to when the entire family was under one roof.

One of the women noticed the cassette player and insisted that Rachel play some film songs for them. They went through her cassettes and saw that she had a collection of old Marathi songs, to which they could not dance. So they brought their own music and danced to the tune of their favourite Hindi film songs. Rachel felt better with the festive mood in her house. She wanted every single woman and child to stay back with her, and, impulsively, invited them to lunch.

Kirtibai laughed, 'My dear friend how will you feed so many mouths? These girls look like ants, but eat like elephants. Now let us see what you have in the kitchen. Three potatoes, two onions, one tomato, ginger, garlic, red chillies, a bunch of coriander leaves, four–five coconuts, and a sackful of Bombay duck. Perhaps you will make a cauldron of your special sol kadhi, no?'

'No,' said Rachel. She stood up, and tucked the end of her sari at her waist, saying, 'Chicken kesari. I will cook it exactly the way I did when I was pregnant with my firstborn.'

Rachel sent for the chicken and started preparations, as the women ran back and forth from their houses, bringing condiments and the food they had cooked in the morning. 'Perhaps we should invite the whole village, in celebration of Rachel's first grandchild,' laughed Kirtibai.

Her words brought tears to Rachel's eyes as she sat chopping the onions. Then, wiping her tears with her arm, she gave the young women the task of preparing the masala. Rachel smiled at the memory of that year, as five of the women who were present there had become pregnant.

She soaked a little saffron in a bowl of warm water. When the chicken was tender, Rachel added the saffron to the chicken and covered the vessel. The rice was almost done in another casserole. By then, the girls had laid out the plates on the drawing room floor. When Rachel opened the lid of the casserole, the fragrance of saffron filled the house.

Rachel watched the younger women in amazement. The colour of their skins had changed to a glowing shade of saffron. And Rachel was sure some of them would become pregnant that night. Their husbands would not be able to keep away from their fragrant bodies.

ANASHI DHAKACHA SAN, PESSACH

Alah ani olah chi pez is made with crushed ginger and lili chay, boiled together till the drink gets a greenish- brown colour. It is strained and served in bowls or glasses, often with a date as a sweetner.

Indian matzo or bin-khameer-chi-bhakhri
Take a cup of wheat flour. Sift; do not add salt. Make a dough, using a little water at a time, divide into four balls and roll into chapattis.

Place a heavy iron griddle or tava on the fire. When hot, lower the flame; roast each chapatti till crisp on both sides.

Matzo bread is the symbol of poverty, as the Jews ate it when they were slaves in the land of Egypt. It is also symbolic of the unleavened bread they carried with them when they fled from Egypt. It inspires Jews to work for freedom, justice and peace.

To make the special bin-khameer-chi-bhakhri for the Seder plate or the Passover platter, roll a chapatti according to the recipe given above; then, with the pressure of the thumb, make a fingertip-sized cap on one side of the chapatti, roast on griddle and keep aside. This cap is symbolic of the priests or Cohens who were allowed to enter the inner sanctum of the temple.

Roll out the second chapatti and make two fingertip- sized m-shaped caps, in memory of the Levis or soldiers.

Then roll the third chapatti and give three rounded fingertip-sized caps, in memory of the Israelis or peasants.

These matzo breads must be kept in a matzo cover on the Seder platter.

Indian sheera or halech or haroset

Soak one kilogram dates overnight, wash, drain, de-seed and cook on a slow fire till soft. Cool and crush dates into a pulp, strain, cook again, lower the heat and continue cooking till the sheera thickens, stirring constantly so that the mixture does not stick to the pan.

Serve in a bowl and place on the Seder platter. Leftover can be kept bottled in the fridge.

Halech or haroset is symbolic of the mortar used by the Jews when they built the pyramids for the Pharaohs.

Jerova

Take the left thighbone of a goat, roast on an open fire and arrange on the Seder plate.

The bone is symbolic of the sacrificial Passover lamb, offered to the lord as thanksgiving when the Jews came to dwell in their ancestral land after many years of wandering.

Optional: roasted leg of chicken.

Karpas-Maror

Bitter herbs or kadu bhaaji, like parsley and salad leaves, are cleaned, washed, dried and placed on the Passover platter with a bowl of lemon juice or limbu cha ras.

Bitter herbs are symbolic of the bitterness and hardships suffered by Jews when they were slaves in Egypt.

Limbu cha ras

Choose fresh lemons, wash, strain the juice, add half teaspoon salt, mix with water in a small bowl so that each person at the table can dip the boiled eggs, parsley and lettuce in the rather salty lime juice. This ritual represents spring and is also symbolic of tears shed as slaves in Egypt.

Boiled egg

For the Seder plate you need one boiled egg, which is roasted on a open fire. You also need an egg per person, to distribute among those present at the Seder table.

Take fresh eggs, washed, hardboiled, shelled and kept in a bowl.

The roasted egg is also symbolic of the sacrificial lamb.

Kiddush

You will need four kilograms black currants to make the required amount of Kiddush sherbet, because each phase in the prayers demands the pouring and drinking of the sherbet or, if possible, wine.

Wash the currants and boil for five minutes in a casserole, strain and pour in jugs or bottles.

Optional: wine!

In mid April, on the first day of Passover, or Pessach, the pale summer moon resembles matzo bread made at home in memory of the Exodus of Jews from Egypt. The passing over from the Dead Sea, and freedom from slavery, is a constant source of inspiration for Jews all over the world, as they pray for deliverance from tyranny, oppression and injustice.

During Passover a traditional Seder table is decorated with flowers, candles, a fresh tablecloth, and a special Pessach platter covered with an embroidered cloth, and the dining table is set with the best tableware—shining, sparkling and festive.

In the mornings, religious Bene Israel Jews drink a concoction called tandla chi pez. The early morning cup of tea with sugar and milk is taboo during Passover, and is substituted with the pez. This drink is made with a handful of broken rice boiled in two cups of water, a pinch of salt and half a cup of coconut milk, cooked till the mixture thickens. It is served in bowls or glasses, often with a date as a sweetner and to be eaten while sipping the pez.

It was Pessach eve.

Rachel sat on the veranda, watching the moon, full and round like a golden platter, resting on the horizon beyond the sea which was deep blue like the shirt Aaron always wore for Pessach prayers.

The soft murmur of the waves reminded Rachel of all the prayers Aaron had conducted with the family. If they celebrated the Pessach eve prayers with the community at the synagogue, they laid the Seder table for the second day in their own house.

Those were endless, happy days. A week ahead of Pessach, every nook and corner of the house was cleaned and all the dishes washed, wiped and put away. A day before Pessach eve Bene Israel women from the surrounding areas would arrive in bullock carts to make the India matzo bread in the courtyard of the synagogue. It resembled their own dry chapattis, not like the roasted crisp matzo that arrived from Israel in well-packed cartons.

For the past many years, Rachel had not set the Seder table with her family. Now that she was alone she prepared a small Seder plate, lit a candle, left a goblet of sherbet for the Prophet Elijah, opened the door for him and sat nibbling at the matzo she had made for herself.

Often she was invited by one of the Alibaug families for the first day's prayers. Her childhood friend Ruby never allowed her to be alone on Pessach nights.

On this particular Pessach, Rachel had declined all invitations. She excused herself, saying she was getting older and the prayers that lasted till midnight tired her.

Watching the moonlight, Rachel told herself that she would prepare a Pessach plate with a chicken bone, a home-made matzo, a boiled egg, a sprig of bitter fenugreek leaves from her backyard and a bowl of date sheera. She would then light a lamp, open the door and leave a glass of wine for the Prophet Elijah; she knew, unseen, he would be there, sitting at her table. Resting on her deckchair, watching the moon and holding a bowl of warm alah ani olah chi pez, Rachel reminisced about those ancient days when the women gathered at the synagogue to make the matzo for the entire community.

Those were days of laughter and happiness. Dressed in colourful saris, jewels and strings of flowers in their hair, the women would arrive early and gather in Rachel's courtyard. They would be carrying their own boards and rolling pins. Rachel would welcome them with hot pez, and the women would then take a leisurely walk along the seashore before returning to the synagogue to make the matzo.

They swept the synagogue and sprinkled water in the courtyard. Then, spreading out the durries on the ground, they washed their hands and settled down to roll the matzo, roasting it on griddles placed on clay stoves. Sometimes, Aaron lit the clay tandoor and spent the entire day roasting matzo breads. The women rolled them out and passed them on to him, as he slapped them inside the oven. When done, he used a wooden spatula to pull them out and throw them on a clean white bed sheet, to be collected by the women and arranged in neat stacks in the storeroom of the synagogue.

While rolling the matzos, one of the women would start humming a kirtan to the Prophet Moses, set to the tune of a popular Marathi kirtan about the birth of Krishna, which was picked up by the others. They sang about the parting of the sea and the Exodus, as the matzos were rolled, roasted, stacked, packed in wicker baskets, covered with cloth and divided equally. Each Jewish family received three special matzos for the Seder platter and a few for the ceremonial meal.

Rachel was not sure whether she wanted to celebrate Pessach this year. Anyway, how does one celebrate the Pessach all alone?

Then she heard the phone ringing inside the house; from the long ring, she knew it was a call from Israel.

The whole family had gathered in Aviv's house to celebrate the Passover: Irene, his wife, grandchildren Tamar and Michael, her second son, Jacob, with his wife, Ilana, and Zephra. They all spoke to her. Zephra was the last to come on the line. She wanted the recipe for Indian matzo.

Rachel gave her a step-by-step instruction. 'Take some wheat flour. Do you have some?'

She could hear Zephra ask Irene, 'Do we have some flour?'

Then she said, 'Yes, we have flour. Now what?'

'It is very simple, but how come you are interested in cooking? In India you refused to even boil an egg!'

Rachel ached for her daughter as she heard her tinkling laughter. 'People change Mama,' she said. 'But do not have high hopes. This is just for Pessach. I am bored of eating this factory-made stuff. Just feeling homesick for your food.'

Rachel was touched by the warmth in her words and told her, 'Take some wheat flour, mix it quickly with water. You need to make a stiff dough, roll it immediately and roast on a griddle.

The rule is, never let the dough stand, and never mix salt, because that is how we took the dough out of Egypt.'

'Tov,' said Zephra, 'and what next, we have some bottled kharoset—'

'What is that?'

'Don't bother Mama, I just remembered you used to make something with dates. We ate it like a sandwich with the matzo. It had an Indian name . . . what was it?'

'Sheera.'

'Yes,' Zephra shouted enthusiastically.

'You cannot make it instantly.'

'Why?'

'Oh Zephra! You haven't changed at all. Always in a mad hurry.'

'Yes, Mama, I want to make it right now.'

'You cannot.'

'Why?'

'Because you have to soak the dates overnight and wait.'

'That means I cannot make it now.'

'Try.'

'How?'

'Take some dates, de-seed them, wash them, cook in a little water on a slow fire till you puree them.'

'That sounds great, because Irene has a packet of seedless dates, the best of Israel.' Then her voice softened. 'What are doing for Pessach, Mama? Going to Alibaug to Aunt Ruby's place?'

Rachel tried to keep her tone even. 'No, nowhere.'

'Oh Mama, I wish you would come here.'

'Zephra,' said Rachel sternly, 'we have discussed this topic a thousand and one times. Nako. Now don't worry about me and have a happy Pessach. You know all the prayers and songs, *daay daay enu* . . .' She was singing, tears running down her face.

'I love you Mama,' said Zephra softly and passed on the phone to Jacob. Rachel sensed they were all thinking about her and also worrying that she was alone in India.

As soon as Jacob came on the line, she told him, 'Tell everybody not to worry about me. I am fine. Also tell them, I am very busy. You know why—because of the synagogue. The committee wants to sell the land and I need some legal advice. Remember you had a friend who used to study law? He often came to Danda with you to spend his summer vacations. Tell me, what was the name of that friend of yours? That tall, lean boy with green eyes who was an atheist.'

'I think you are talking about Judah.'

'Do you have his phone number?'

'Now?'

'Yes, now.'

'I don't have it on me. But I can tell you where to look for his number. In our house.'

'Our house? Where?'

'Danda. Where else?' Jacob said, laughing.

'Where shall I look?'

'In the old black phone book. The one you keep under the telephone. I keep all my Indian phone numbers there, open it and look under J.'

'OK.'

'Don't tell me you are going to call him now?'

'Why not?'

'OK, then look for J for Judah and the Bombay code number. Most probably you will find him home. I doubt if he is celebrating Pessach like everybody else.'

'Well, I will call him tomorrow for the second day of Pessach. Then I have reason to cook.'

'Do not make it too religious. He is sort of strange.'

'I will remember your advice. Good night and eat well.'

Before Jacob could say anything, Rachel had hung up, found the tattered old telephone diary and started looking for Judah's number.

The phone kept ringing for full five minutes before Judah answered. He sounded as if he was in a hurry. Rachel immediately came to the point. 'Allo,' she said, 'I am Rachel. Remember me?'

'No,' he said rather brusquely.

'Let me remind you, I am Jacob's mother from Danda. He now lives in Israel.'

Judah softened as he said, 'Yes, Aunty Rachel, I remember you.'

Rachel relaxed. 'Judah, I need to meet you, as soon as possible.'

She could feel his smile. 'How can I help you?'

'I have a problem.'

'What sort of problem?'

'Legal. I believe you are a lawyer?'

'Yes, I am.'

'That is it. I need your advice.'

'What sort of advice?'

'You know we have a synagogue in Danda—right behind the house?'

'Yes, I remember seeing it from the outside.'

'Well, I look after the synagogue and am very attached to it. But the synagogue committee wants to sell it with the land around it to some Chinoy-Finoy, who wants to make a beach resort and also grow flowers here.'

'Yes . . .'

'And, I do not want them to sell the synagogue or the land. So I need your help. How do we meet?'

'Do you come to Bombay?'

'Yes, sometimes.'

'Then, why don't you come here next Monday? I could receive you at the ten o'clock catamaran at the Gateway of India.'

'No son, I cannot come. I want you to come here, so that you can see the synagogue.'

'All right, I can come to Danda. I haven't been there in years. Tell me when?'

'Tomorrow.'

Rachel heard him leafing through his diary, saying, 'I have an appointment tomorrow afternoon. It is not important. I could cancel it.'

'Why don't you come by noon and stay for dinner?'

'No, thank you Aunty. I would like to return to Bombay by evening.'

'Even on the Passover? Are you invited somewhere?'

'I do not . . . have not . . . I would like to come, but I live alone. I do not know any prayers. No family. Nothing.'

Judah felt comforted when she said softly, 'We will just eat together.'

'Aunty, I will be there tomorrow, say around three or four.'

'Thank you son. I will wait for you.'

Putting the phone back on the cradle, she went to the kitchen and soaked a handful of dates in one bowl, a handful of black currants in another, and heaved a sigh of relief.

The next day, when Judah arrived, Rachel saw that he was not the same person she had known. He appeared to be leaner, taller in his blue jeans and white tee shirt. The green eyes behind the thick black-rimmed spectacles looked greener. He gave her a warm handshake and a hug. He was not at all cold and distant, as she had expected him to be. He inquired about Jacob and the rest of the family. But when she asked about his family, there was silence. Rachel did not force him but she vaguely remembered that his grandfather had been cremated, much to the shock of the Jewish community. Since then, his family had maintained a distance from the Jewish community. A Jew had to be buried, so that it was easy to wake up from the dead and welcome the Messiah.

At the synagogue, Judah made detailed notes and asked pointed questions. His face was expressionless and he did not give Rachel any hope. By the evening Rachel was rather annoyed with his silence. The only time she saw his face change was when she opened the door of the synagogue. Judah hesitated, as Rachel kissed the mezuzah. His hands were hanging awkwardly at his sides and she saw that he was not a practising Jew.

He studied its design in great detail and after a deep breath entered the synagogue and stood staring at the high ceiling and chandeliers. He looked like someone who had rarely been inside a synagogue. Even if he was impressed, he did not show it. Rachel was surprised, but kept her silence.

Back in the house, she offered him a bowl of strong pez of ginger and mint and went to the kitchen to prepare the Passover dinner. Even if he was used to tea and needed it, out of respect for her feelings, he did not say anything. Later, watching him from the kitchen, Rachel was surprised to see him sitting cross-legged on the floor of the veranda with a pen in hand and notebook resting on his knee. It was then that Rachel started warming to him.

She sat next to him on the floor, de-seeding the dates.

Judah asked her for the names of committee members and people associated with the synagogue. Rachel noticed that he used a heavy felt pen and wrote in a big hand. Once the dates were ready, Rachel went back to the kitchen to cook the sheera.

She was standing at the kitchen platform and stirring the sheera when Judah came into the kitchen asking if she remembered the date when the synagogue was last used. Quickly she said, 'How can I forget a day like that? That was when Jacob's father closed his eyes and departed for his heavenly abode and we did his seven-day ceremony there.' Rachel choked back her tears as she pretended to look at the sheera. She felt Judah's comforting touch on her shoulders. 'Aunty, can you tell me why we make the halech on Passover night?'

With eyes moist, she looked up at him and smiled. 'I am glad you know the Hebrew word for sheera and that you asked me this question.'

Judah slid the notebook in his pocket and listened carefully. Rachel poured the mixture into a crystal bowl while explaining, 'I am not educated like you, but I can tell you what I used to tell my children. This is in memory of the mortar we used when we were slaves and were making the pyramids in Egypt.'

He was looking at her intently. 'My parents were not practising Jews, but we always had the Seder service.'

Respecting his privacy, Rachel did not ask him anything about his mother. She was sure that by the end of the evening he would open his own book of life. As a mother, she knew that if she wanted to get closer to him she was not to ask him any questions. When children wanted to say something, they clamped down if asked questions.

She felt a great love for this young man who was like one of her sons, but a little different. Weird, Jacob had said.

That morning, Rachel had made the matzo breads and kept them covered with a silk cloth. The rest were kept aside for dinner. Rachel rarely ate in the dining room; the veranda was her dining-cum-living room. But with Judah in the house, she decided to use the dining room, spreading an embroidered tablecloth for the Seder plate, new plates, crystal goblets and a bottle of wine Judah had brought for the Passover dinner.

She saw the look of dread on Judah's face when she lit the candle and smiled, 'This is to remember the Prophet Elijah.'

Judah opened the bottle of wine and asked for the Prophet's glass, a ruby-red goblet, which Rachel had kept aside for the Prophet Elijah. She knew he would join them tonight.

Judah poured the wine, stood up and opened the door for the Prophet, sat down and clinked glasses with Rachel, saying 'le haim,' as a toast to life. Rachel was pleased. They sipped the wine with matzo, halech, greens and the egg dipped in salt water.

Feeling warm and jubilant, Rachel told him about all her children, her life in Danda, her neighbours and how her world revolved around the synagogue. Judah told her about his work, the sort of cases he had fought and some funny anecdotes related to his cases.

But not once did he speak about his family.

As they finished more than half a bottle of wine, Rachel served a rich mutton pulao, their Passover dinner. After dinner, Judah was adamant about helping Rachel put everything away in the kitchen. Although she insisted that her maid would do the dishes the next day, he persisted with washing the plates, glasses, bowls and goblets, saying his mother never allowed the maids to touch the precious festive glassware. As Rachel made his bed in Jacob's room, Judah sat on the veranda, watching the sea. He could hear Rachel humming a Marathi kirtan about Moses crossing the sea and felt he had returned home.

The bed made, Rachel called out to Judah. He stood towering over her, saying, 'Don't worry, Aunty, together we will overcome everything.'

A silver beam seemed to be cutting through the sea. Perhaps the Prophet Moses had parted the waters and they would Passover together.

BOMBAY DUCK

Ingredients: bombil, oil, chilli powder, turmeric, salt, rice flour or gram flour

Most Bene Israel Jews are very fond of Bombay duck or bombil. It is a small eel-like fish, rather soft and fleshy with a red head, the colour of which indicates its freshness. Bombils are sun-dried, salted and stored, so that they are always handy to make a quick dinner, or as an accompaniment to khichdi on Saturday night, when the Sabbath ends.

This fish has one bone and has to be gutted delicately. The fine white scales have to be scraped and the head can be left on or chopped off; the fish is then halved and salted. Excess salt and water are removed by keeping the fish under a weight, preferably a stone pestle. It helps to flatten out the bombil and squeeze out all moisture.

When dry, the fish is cleaned with lemon and salt, coated with rice flour mixed with salt, turmeric, a dash of chilli powder, and shallow fried till golden brown.

The rice flour coating makes the fish crisp and crunchy.

➤◆➤

Rachel felt crushed, like a bombil weighed under a stone pestle. Drained of all emotion, she was feeling depressed and annoyed that Mr Chinoy and the committee had taken to driving around the synagogue. The committee members did not phone her or inform her of their intended arrival as they normally did. They did not even ask her for the synagogue keys. They did not want to see it from the inside; they were only interested in the land. Once they even brought a plan and she saw Mr Chinoy's engineer making drawings and taking measurements.

Whenever she saw Chinoy's car, her heart sank. She was also angry that Mordecai and the other committee members did not stop by the house to greet her. From their comings and goings, Rachel understood that something was happening under a veil of secrecy. She was angry at their indifferent behaviour and that they did not even bother to acknowledge her presence. She was certain Mr Chinoy was serving them breakfast, lunch and drinks and sending them back to Bombay in his fancy car.

Much to her resentment, Chinoy would step out of the car dressed in a white suit and dark glasses.

Her eyes followed each and every bend in the road with insult and injury writ large on her face.

At the end of two months, there was a knock at her door one morning. Instinctively she knew they had come visiting. When she opened the door, she saw Mordecai with the whole committee and Mr Chinoy. Mordecai was grinning. Rachel noticed that all his teeth had fallen except one on the right.

There was a woman with Mr Chinoy. Perhaps she was Mrs Chinoy. Rachel understood that today they would make all possible effort to beguile her into selling her property. She welcomed them politely and offered them the chairs she always kept on the veranda, holding on to her own.

Rachel noticed that Mrs Chinoy was stylish but had a kind face. She was wearing sports shoes, a grey tracksuit, a striped magenta scarf thrown over her shoulders and her dark glasses pushed back over her long, black hair. Rachel did not expect her to speak in Marathi, but she did, calling her aunty, appreciating the house and complimenting Rachel on her youthful looks.

Rachel was rather annoyed, wondering why they were making small talk and not coming to the point. It was obvious that it was a business trip. Mr Chinoy sat thinking and did not say anything, while Mordecai sheepishly proposed that if she ever wanted to sell her property Mr Chinoy would happily buy it for his beach resort, as they were finalizing the deal about the synagogue.

Rachel said, 'Nako,' rather abruptly and sat straight in her chair, staring into space. Mrs Chinoy noticed her reaction and tried to change the subject by inviting her to their farmhouse in Alibaug.

Sitting still, Rachel did not answer. Instead she asked if they would have some limbu paani.

Mr Chinoy saw the look of determination on her face and accepted her invitation for a drink. She resembled his mother and he did not want to push her too far.

Mrs Chinoy helped her pass around the glasses. When they finished their drink, Chinoysaab bowed and took her leave with an elaborate thank you and Mrs Chinoy held her hands, saying she would return to spend time with her. On her way out, she noticed the sacks of dry bombil kept on the veranda and said, 'I believe the Bene Israels make excellent Bombay duck.'

With unusual enthusiasm, Mordecai immediately ran back, saying, 'Yes, madam, Rachel sister's bombils are extraordinary. When her husband was . . .' Rachel froze him with a stare.

Mrs Chinoy shook her head appreciatively and asked, 'Perhaps you could teach me how to make them. I love fried bombils, but can never get them right. I had this friend in school who always brought some for me. Perhaps one day you will teach me. I could come over and watch you cook.'

Rachel gave her a tight smile. 'I will send you a message when I get fresh bombils, but I don't have your phone number.'

Mrs Chinoy pulled out a card from her bag and gave it to Rachel. She then pulled down her dark glasses over her beautiful grey eyes and disappeared behind the shaded glass of her air-conditioned car.

As Rachel saw the car disappear, her momentary pleasure turned to anguish. She was consumed by the desire to tell Mrs Chinoy that no amount of maska was going to force her to sell the house and she would save the synagogue at all costs from that shark-like husband of hers.

She was so agitated that she needed to speak to Judah at that very moment. She called him and felt angry with frustration when he said he was with a client and would call her back in an hour.

'What am I to do for an hour?' Rachel asked herself and walked the length and breadth of the veranda, till she slumped in her chair, dry and lifeless like a bombil hanging on the fisherwoman's line.

By the time Judah called, Rachel was at her wit's end. She gave him the details about the visit. Judah did not say anything. Rachel thought he was not listening and asked harshly, 'Judah, are you there? I need your advice.'

'Yes Aunty. I am listening.'

'This Chinoy-Finoy was here with that slimy Mordecai. He wants to buy my house.'

'Do you want to sell it?'

'No.'

'Did they understand that?'

'Yes.'

'So the message is clear.'

'I am not worried about that.'

'Then what is the problem? If it is your house, they cannot take it from you.'

'That is true. But what about the synagogue?'

'Aunty, I really do not know, but perhaps you could lose it.'

'How can you say something like that?'

'Because I made inquiries and the committee has the full power to lease the land around the synagogue.'

'So, what next?'

'Do you have any papers?'

'What papers?'

'Papers about the synagogue.'

'No, but there is a big bundle of books in the synagogue, tied up in a cloth and kept in the cupboard. Nobody ever touches them and I am sure they are infested with silver fish and white ants.'

'Did the committee ever ask for these books?'

'No, I think they have forgotten all about them.'

'Could you bring these books to your house?'

'I can. When do you want them?'

'Next Saturday, I will come and go through them.'

'Can't you come a little earlier, before Saturday?'

'I can try, but it looks difficult.'

'Try.'

'I will. But I have one more question.'

'Like what?'

'Did they ask you for the keys to the synagogue?'

'No.'

'Where are the keys?'

'Right here, tied to my sari.'

Rachel heard a strange sound at the other end of the line. It was Judah, laughing.

With a smile in her voice, she said, 'You must laugh more often. I already feel better. But tell me why you are laughing.'

'Because you keep the keys tied to your sari.'

'Not only that,' she said, 'I even sleep with them.'

His voice turned serious as he said, 'You must really love your synagogue.'

Rachel felt a sob rise in her throat. 'Yes,' she whispered.

On Saturday when Judah arrived, Rachel left him on the veranda with the books she had carried to the house from the synagogue. The pages were tattered, torn, fragile, in fragments and full of silver fish. He went through all the papers, drinking endless cup of tea, until he finally found an old resolution made by an earlier committee, which said that the synagogue could not be sold.

He called out to Rachel, jubilantly waving the paper at her, while she was feeding her hens in the courtyard. 'Aunty, look what I found. Perhaps we can save your precious synagogue.'

Rachel smiled, 'If that is true, wait till I finish feeding these silly birds and then I will get you a box of sweets.'

Then, calling out to the fishmonger's son, she asked him to get her some sweets from Somu, who made fresh coconut chikkis down the road. The boy broke into a run and returned with a packet. Rachel gave a few to the child, offered some to Judah, broke a piece for herself and ate it with obvious pleasure.

But pleasure turned to irritation when Judah looked at her earnestly and asked, 'But before we go ahead with this, if you win the case, what do I get in return, as my fees?'

'Fees?' Rachel was dumbfounded; she had never thought about such practical matters and was not sure whether it was meant to be a joke.

So she said the first thing that came to her mind. 'I have nothing, but perhaps the children could pay you your fees. As for me, all I have is a daughter. I can offer her hand in marriage to you.'

Halfway through her sentence, Rachel saw a flash of anger on his face and the next thing she knew he had dashed out of the house. She ran after him, apologizing, but even before she could reach the wicket gate, he had climbed in an autorickshaw and disappeared up the road.

With a sinking heart, Rachel picked up the books and papers, tied them up in an old tablecloth and put them away. Then she started wondering what her mistake was. In the old days, if she said a thing like that, nobody would ever take it as an offence.

It was a normal sort of joke. But then she realized that perhaps she had said something she should not have. Even her daughter did not like such jokes. More so because Judah never spoke about himself or even his family. She should not have said something so personal. Rachel was not sure if he had seen her daughter or how old Zephra was when he came to the house with Jacob. She scolded herself for making such a silly mistake, but was nevertheless surprised that he could not take a joke. For that matter, even she was dumb when it came to jokes. Perhaps he was just joking when he asked for his fees?

On his way to the Alibaug harbour to catch the catamaran back to Bombay, Judah regretted his action. He should not have rushed out of Rachel's house like that. After all, she was a traditional woman and did not realize that he was hypersensitive about a topic like marriage. How was she to know that he did not like this particular subject? He had half a mind to return to Danda, but by then he was so irritable that, when he saw the catamaran, all he wanted to do was go back home.

Rachel snatched a handful of Bombay duck from the sack on the veranda and soaked them in a bowl of water. Then she quickly dressed in a simple sari with brown checks and a black border and returned to the kitchen to make fried bombils for Judah. She knew the way to a man's heart was through his stomach, and she would definitely reach it. She had come to love him, like her own son.

The bombil had softened in the water. She coated them with rice flour and fried them to a rich golden brown. Leaving them to drain on a paper napkin, Rachel powdered her face, applied a few drops of eau de cologne to her throbbing temples, packed the fish in a steel dabba and took some karanjias always kept in a tin on the kitchen shelf. On her way out, Rachel picked up the telephone diary and locked the house, found an autorickshaw and requested the driver to rush to the Alibaug harbour. She had to catch the last catamaran to Bombay.

In the catamaran, she sat on the edge of her seat, worried and tense. What if he was not at home? What if she did not find him? Where would she spend the night? Perhaps she would have to phone her Santa Cruz cousins. As darkness fell upon the sea, her heart sank and she covered her shoulders with the end of her sari. Then she felt the warmth of the Bombay duck on her knee and was sure that the fish would lead her to Judah.

During the forty-five-minute ride, Rachel rehearsed her dialogue with Judah. She needed a good opening sentence. She was even willing to say sorry, if necessary.

Soon she found herself thinking about the word 'Bombay duck'. Why did it have a name like that? Why was it a staple diet of the Jews? Had the ancestors discovered that it was as sweet as the salmon they had known in the Promised Land? Or was it the perfect choice when one needed a quick recipe for a Saturdaynight dinner, when Sabbath ended and heralded the beginning of a new week?

It was dark when Rachel reached Bombay. As soon as she got off the catamaran, she found a phone booth, opened her telephone diary and dialled Judah's number. He did not answer immediately.

She panicked; perhaps he was not at home. She felt ridiculous, standing there with the box of bombils. Disappointed, she was about to hang up, when Judah answered. Overcome with emotion, she could not say anything as he kept on repeating his hellos, his impatience rising.

With difficulty she managed to say, 'Judah. It's me. Rachel.' She spoke so softly that he took some time to realize that it was Rachel. She was relieved that he did not sound irritable; instead he was worried about her well-being and apologetic. 'Aunty, I am so sorry I left in a temper. You shouldn't have come all the way. Please, please stay where you are. I will pick you up in half an hour.'

Sitting on a bench and watching a balloon seller, Rachel was thinking, 'Now, why did he say he was sorry, when I am the one who should be sorry?'

Judah arrived in his small Fiat, and ran towards her with open arms. She gave him a hug and wiped her tears with the end of her sari. Judah drove Rachel to his flat near Bombay Central. It was an old housing society in a tree-lined lane. As he opened the lock, Rachel stood hesitating, clutching at the box of bombil, and then offered it to him saying, 'Something I made for you.'

'So soon! Because I think you took the next catamaran after mine. You hardly had any time to cook. If I hadn't returned home for a wash, you wouldn't have found me. And what would you have done in big bad Bombay in the middle of the night? I was about to go out and find myself something to eat.'

Opening the box, he said, 'Bombil!'

Rachel smiled indulgently as he waved a hand at the mess that was his house. 'This is where I live, a bachelor's den. I use the front room as my office. Look at all these papers and files. This one is supposed to be my drawing-cum-dining-room-cum-kitchen, where I just make tea or a sandwich. And that is my bedroom. Pandu comes in the morning to clean and wash my clothes. Sometimes, ifl am sick, he makes me some khichdi,' he said rolling his eyes. 'The perfect combination with bombil-batata, nako?'

'Right,' said Rachel as she sat down on a chair. 'Now, will you please allow me to say something?'

'No, no Aunty, don't tell me you want to apologize. Because I know you were joking, but I am so irritable about marriage that I react like a madman.'

'Why?'

'I will tell you the whole story some other time. But before that let us eat.'

'If you have some dal and rice, I can make khichdi.'

'No, no, you must be tired. You have come all the way just to pacify this stupid temper of mine. You stay right here, while I get some food packed from the restaurant downstairs.'

When Judah returned with two plates of bhaaji-pau, Rachel was looking at the photographs on the walls. She had noticed that he had inherited the green eyes from his beautiful mother and his father was a handsome man with a square jaw. His grandfather looked like a small man and his grandmother appeared to tower over him.

Judah introduced each one of them to Rachel and said, 'All dead.'

'Any brothers and sisters?'

'One sister. She lives in Canada with her family. Haven't seen her in years.'

They had a cosy dinner, sitting in the balcony. Judah was happy and satisfied as he put away the plates and then sat smoking in the dark. He asked, 'Aunty, what does your daughter do?'

Far away from Danda and Israel, Rachel smiled at the memory of her daughter. 'Zephra. She is an Israeli. She lives on a kibbutz. I worry about her. But what can I do? Except worry. She is preparing for an exam to study archaeology.'

'I remember her in pigtails. She was sort of tall for her age.'

Afraid of another misunderstanding, Rachel changed the subject, asking, 'Tell me, do you think we can save the synagogue?'

'We will try, nako?' He smiled.

That night, as Rachel curled up in Judah's bed, he sat next to her, holding her hand and telling her why he was uncomfortable with Jewish rituals. Since his grandfather had chosen to be cremated, the community had ostracized his family.

Yet, his mother had given him a proper Jewish upbringing by following all the traditions and festivals, which they celebrated at home. Their infrequent visits to the synagogue had left him feeling bitter. He had been in his early thirties when his mother died, leaving him alienated in both societies, Indian and Jewish.

Judah switched off the lights; he did not want her to see the expression on his face. That night, all he wanted her to do was listen.

Then he carried his mattress to the other room and closed the door behind him. Rachel felt comforted to be with him under the same roof. She did not have to be alone with tbe night-sounds of Danda.

The next morning, bathed, dressed and ready to leave, Rachel woke him up with a cup of tea. He smiled, saying, 'Just like Mama.'

Later, at the Gateway of India, Rachel climbed into the catamaran on her way back to Danda, and turned around to Judah, smiling. 'And what about your fees?'

'Bombil-batata and moong dal khichdi!'

TANDLYA CHI BHAKHRI

Ingredients: rice flour, water, oil, salt

Method: Boil two cups of water with half a teaspoon salt, reduce the flame and slowly mix with two cups of flour, stirring continuously and making sure there are no lumps. Remove from fire to a thali and knead into dough while still warm. Divide into small balls with oily hands, roll into chapattis and roast lightly on a griddle. Serve hot with mint chutney, pickle, vegetables or a curry, preferably green.

❖

Rice is the symbol of fertility. After the wedding, the bride is showered with rice and confetti, so that she becomes the mother of many children.

Rice is the staple diet of most Bene Israel Jews. A Bene Israel meal is never complete without rice.

On the way back to Danda, Rachel was happy.

The paddy fields around the house looked fresh and green, like the sari she had worn during her mehndi ceremony, the day before her wedding.

When she reached home, Rachel was hungry and knew exactly what she wanted to eat: rice chapattis. But before that she had to feed Brownie, the cat, the goat and the birds. Normally she fed them early in the morning. Today for a change she had not been there to attend to their needs.

Quickly she took some milk from the fridge and fed Brownie and the cat, threw some fodder to the goat and refilled the bowls of millet for the birds.

She then had a quick bath, changed into a much-worn sari, white with a green border; old saris were soft and comforting.

In the fridge were bottled chutneys and a bowl of kheer she had made the day before, but she did not feel like eating any of it. Instead she made rice chapattis and decided to eat them with some coriander chutney she had made earlier.

With plate on lap, she sat on the veranda, eating her frugal lunch. Everything matched: her mood, her sari. Even the sea looked green. Just like the fish curry she used to make for the children. Fondly she remembered that Zephra loved it so much that she had it like a soup.

Lately, Zephra had taken to asking her for all sorts of recipes on the phone. Rachel was surprised and wondered if she was in love with one of those Israeli boys in the photographs Zephra had sent her. Rachel knew that when daughters started asking for recipes they always had a reason, but perhaps Zephra was just homesick.

Missing her, Rachel had a strong desire to speak to her. Zephra was excited to hear her mother's voice. 'Oh Mama,' she said, 'you gave me such a scare. Are you sick or something—because you rarely call.'

'I just wanted to speak to you.'

'Yes,' she laughed, 'but no marriage topics.'

'You young people are terrible about simple matters. In our days, it was natural to talk about such things and we never took offence.'

'Marriage, is it a simple matter?'

'Nako.'

'I am so glad you called, okay? For a change you can advice me about marriage.'

'No, this is not about your marriage,' said Rachel sternly, 'this is about our synagogue.'

'Is that where you want to get me married?'

'No.'

'What about the synagogue? The last time I was there, remember, we cleaned it together? It must be a ruin by now.'

'Yes, it is in bad shape, but I am going to save it.'

'From what?'

'From some evil people.'

'What sort of evil people?'

'The synagogue committee.'

'Ah, like Uncle Mordecai and others, right?' laughed Zephra.

'Yes, you have a good memory. They have made a pact with a man called Chinoy-Finoy, I forget his name.'

'Who is that?'

'A shark, who wants to buy up all possible land here and make seaside resorts.'

'Isn't he the same man who has a farm near Alibaug? The last time I was home, I saw his nameplate and a hoarding about exotic flowers and beach resorts . . .'

'Yes, that is the man, a smart businessman. What does he know about synagogues, tradition, ritual, sentiment and attachment? For him it is just prime land, not a religious place. But I must give him credit for not pushing too hard. He has left the decision to the committee, if they want to sell it or lease it. What a shame! Most of these committee members were circumcised here, had their bar mitzvah here and even married here. And now they want to sell the house of our Lord. The last time they were here, they were trying to convince me that they want to use the money for the development of the community. Big fat stories. I am so disgusted.'

'But, Mama, I suppose the committee can take a decision to sell a synagogue or keep it. Why are you so upset?'

'Upset is not the right word. I am suffering, because they have the audacity to make a business out of religion.'

'But, Mama, nobody uses the synagogue any more. When did you last have services there?'

'Ah, they don't want to do anything there. Before Chinoy-Finoy made this offer, they used to come here and talk about saving our heritage. Since they have an offer from Mr Orchidwallah, all they think about is money. Wonder how they are going to use all that money! Because everybody has left for Israel, we are just a handful here in India.'

'What-wallah did you say?'

'Arre, this Orchidwallah.'

Zephra giggled. 'Mama, you are funny.'

'Why should I not be upset? The other day, they came here, the whole lot of them and asked me if I wanted to sell our house. Chinoy-Finoy was ready to buy it right away.'

'How dare they say something like that to Rachel Dandekar?'

'They did. I was so angry. Just kept sitting in my chair. When they were about to leave, I thought I was being rude, so offered them some limbu paani.'

'Mama, you are the limit.' Zephra was laughing. 'So what did you say?'

'That is not the end of my story. Because they even brought this woman to irritate me.'

'What woman?'

'Mrs Chinoy-Finoy, who else?'

'Why did she annoy you?'

'She is this typical very Bombaiya woman dressed in sports clothes and all that.'

'What do you mean by Bombaiya?'

'A typical Bombay girl. She even tried to blackmail me emotionally.'

'Now, how is that possible? How can anybody blackmail you?'

'She was smart, trying to be affectionate, saying, aunty this and aunty that, aunty will you please teach me how to make bombils? Aunty you are so beautiful, your skin is so smooth, it is difficult to guess your age. Now, don't I know that I look like a dry bombil! Then, when she had nothing better to say, she kept on complimenting me about the house and all that nonsense. Does she think I am a child, who will be carried away by her sweet chatter? So, I said, come again some other day, I will teach you how to make bombils.'

'Will you?'

'Teach her? Nako.'

'So, what are you doing, selling the house?'

'No, I am not selling the house, nor will I allow them to sell the synagogue.'

'How can you stop them from selling the synagogue?'

'Just wait and see, I will.'

'Is anybody helping you?'

'Yes, Judah.'

'Judah who?'

'Do you remember, on Pessach eve you called me for the recipe for sheera? That night, I had asked Jacob for a phone number.'

'So, who is this Judah?'

'A friend of Jacob's who used to spend his vacations with us. You were just a teenager then. I wonder if you remember him— that tall boy with glasses and green eyes. He was studying law.'

'That green-eyed monster?'

'Yes, he is one of Bombay's best lawyers. But why do you call him a monster?'

'Arre, don't you remember how rude he was? If we offered him something, he would grunt and refuse. Once he told me, don't serve me. Since then, if you remember, I refused to even look at him.'

'He is still like that, sort of rough.'

'Then, how do you work with him?'

'In a way he is very affectionate.'

'I cannot believe it. Tell me Mama, do you need me there?'

'No. If there is anything, I will tell you.'

'Mama, I cannot believe you have this activist streak in you. Why don't you leave India and come here?' Zephra's voice was sweet like honey.

'Nako,' said Rachel, 'when I die, bury me next to your father.'

'Mama, you upset me.'

'Sorry darling.'

'How can I help you?'

'Judah is working on this case and wants to involve the Bene Israel Jews of Israel to create public opinion. Can you help?'

'I can. Call me back in a week. I will speak to some people here and let you know.'

'A week?' Rachel exclaimed.

'Why?'

'I have no time.'

'You won't be late, Mama. Even Chinoy-Finoys take ages to make land deals.'

Rachel felt better after speaking to Zephra. She told her everything, but did not dare tell her how she had almost offered her hand in marriage to Judah, without her permission.

That night, Judah called Rachel. He made kind inquiries about her trip back to Danda. Much to her pleasure, he sounded affectionate and concerned. He told her, 'I have been thinking about you and the synagogue. I even read some books and have come to the conclusion that, before we do anything else, we need public opinion.'

'Did you say anything like that when I was in Bombay?'

'Like what?'

'I thought you said something about public opinion. Somehow, the words keep playing in my mind.'

'No, I never said it.'

'I thought you did, because I was just speaking to my daughter and told her we needed to create public opinion.'

'I did not tell you that, but it is a brilliant idea. How did you think about it?'

'Arre, nothing, it is not my idea. I am just repeating your words.'

'Tell me Aunty, can your family really create public opinion in Israel?'

'I do not promise. All I can do is speak to them and try.'

'So, start working on that right away.'

She liked the sound of hope in his voice. Perhaps, together they would save the synagogue.

That night, as she fell asleep, Rachel was trying to figure out how and when she had heard the term 'public opinion'. Who had whispered it in her ear? Was it the Prophet Elijah sitting next to her in the catamaran, on her way back to Danda?

INDIAN OMELETTE

Ingredients: eggs, onion, green chilli, ginger, garlic, tomato, salt, coriander leaves, oil, ghee or butter

Method: Break two eggs in a bowl and beat till fluffy. Chop one small onion, a tomato, a small piece of ginger, one flake garlic, one green chilli and a few coriander leaves.

Heat one tablespoon oil in a frying pan or a non-stick pan, and brown onion. Add tomato, ginger, garlic, chilli, coriander and salt. Remove from fire and fold in the eggs. Mix well.

Reheat the frying pan, pour the egg mixture, lift the pan and allow the egg to spread out on the pan. Fry omelette on one side, then the other.

When golden brown on both sides, lift with spatula and serve hot with a fresh loaf of bread or chapattis.

Variation: Add half teaspoon gram flour to the mixture before frying the omelette.

The omelette can be folded into a triangle before serving.

❦

The egg is a symbol of life, womb, fertility and the creation of life.

When Judah returned to Danda, there was a spring in his step as he entered Rachel's house. Brownie the dog, the goat and the cat now recognized him. If the goat and the cat acknowledged his presence with a flick of their ears, Brownie rushed up to him, barking and wagging his tail.

As he carried Brownie into the house, Rachel smiled. 'I saw you coming. How did you know that I was making besan laddoos?'

'Aunty, these fragrances follow me wherever I go. I have to just close my eyes and think of you. And, believe me, I know what you are cooking. Today, I knew it was going to be besan laddoos!'

'You mean, you are going to stay for lunch?' teased Rachel.

'Of course. Earlier I was shy and kept on asking for those innumerable cups of tea. But not any more.'

Judah had written a detailed report about the synagogue, which would help generate public opinion among the Jews of India and Israel. He had also contacted Mordecai and asked for a copy of the trust deed of the synagogue. He had a list of the names of the trustees and other committee members with him and was contacting each one of them personally. Rachel was pleased to know that Judah had discovered that not all members were in favour of leasing out the synagogue or its premises. According to the trust deed, the committee did not have the authority to sell the land.

Judah made himself comfortable in a severe straight-backed chair with hand rests. As a rule, he never sat on Rachel's deckchair. She kept an assortment of mismatched chairs, which had come down to her from her ancestors, Abraham, Solomon, Bathsheba, Menashe, Enoch, Shlumith, Joseph and Simha. She had asked the village carpenter to repair all the broken chairs that had been stored on the mezzanine for years.

Now, repaired, coloured, polished, padded with plastic or textiles, or woven with fine cane and strewn with colourful cushions that Rachel had embroidered with floral designs and words like 'welcome', 'greetings', 'shalom' and 'good night', they looked like expensive antique furniture. Rachel and Judah spent many a peaceful afternoon on the veranda, discussing the numerous intricate problems related to the synagogue. Rachel was sure that her ancestors were also sitting there on their respective chairs and listening to them.

In the afternoon, Rachel rested under the awning of the veranda and, automatically as if at a signal, the cat curled up on her cushion. The dog preferred to sit under Rachel's chair, the goat sat still on a bed of grass, the ducks dozed under the lantana bushes near the pond and the hens retired to their coops.

Rachel often wondered how people who have not known each other before became close, like family members. Sometimes, bonds of love were built without effort. When Judah had first walked into Rachel's house, he had appeared lone and distant and she had never imagined that he would become close to her, like a son.

As she shaped the besan laddoos in her palms, she started worrying that there was no bread in the house and she was not in a mood to make chapattis. She had planned to make an omelette for lunch and have a laddoo for dessert. She kept the laddoos in a dabba on the dining table. Returning to the kitchen, she started to make the omelette.

She stood at the kitchen window, wondering if she should make a chapatti for Judah or just serve him a plain omelette with a bowl of ball curry, which she had kept frozen in the fridge. Judah solved her problem by opening his briefcase and pulling out a loaf of bread he had brought for her. Rachel's face lit up as she wondered if he had the power of reading her thoughts.

As they ate, Judah explained to her the meaning of public opinion and the legal implications. Rachel was busy thinking of getting more and more people involved in her project.

Eating a laddoo, she said, 'I know exactly how to create public opinion. Let us call Aviv, Jacob and Zephra and ask them to start a signature campaign in Israel. You can send them a letter explaining the exact problem and what we need. Once they have the details, they can speak to the Indian Jews in Israel. If they can convince them, they could collect donations, and then,' she said, taking a deep breath, 'we could buy off the synagogue from the committee.'

Judah started laughing, and corrected her: 'Take it on lease.'

He was amused by her simplicity and enthusiasm. Rachel was talking about it as though it was child's play. He alone knew how complicated it was going to be, to make a case without a base.

With writing pad balanced on his knee, Judah started making notes, asking Rachel, 'Who is the muqadam of the synagogue?'

'How do you know a word like that? Do you know what it means?' Rachel was surprised.

'Yes, the leader or the president of the managing committee of the synagogue.'

'I am impressed,' said Rachel, shaking her head.

'So, tell me who is this muqadam?'

'He is an old porpoise called Jhirad. He is more of a decoration than anything else. Never speaks a word. Just says "yes" to whatever Mordecai suggests.'

'That means Mordecai must be the treasurer or the gabbai. A very important person in the entire set-up.'

'As far as I can remember he has been a gabbai for ever.'

'Tell me, what have you observed about the choglas? What is their role in the functioning of the synagogue?'

'We used to have five active choglas. One of them was my late husband. Once in a while if the hazzan was sick, he even officiated services. He had a good memory and knew all the Hebrew prayers by heart.'

'What about the hazzan? Did you ever have a regular cantor?'

'We had Hassaji Daniyal. He now lives in Alibaug and makes the meat kosher for us. I always buy a little from him on Fridays.

He knows all the prayers and rituals by heart. He can conduct prayers in both languages, Hebrew and Marathi, so that people like me can understand the meaning. But, as a cantor, he earned very little and was living on the charity of the community. Since no regular services are held at the synagogues around here, he lives a hand-to-mouth existence. Do you know what he does for a living? He has an old horse on which he gives joy rides to children on the Alibaug beach.'

'Do you remember how many people attended the services?'

'We were about two hundred Jews from six to seven villages around Danda. We spent a lot of time at the synagogue. What else could one do? Go to see the tamasha? The lavni? The Ramlila? Visit friends? Or even go to the cinema in Alibaug once in a while? Our lives revolved around the synagogue.'

'Did you have a shamash, the traditional messenger?'

'Yes, we had a messenger, a shamash who also did odd jobs at the synagogue.'

'Do you remember his name?'

'Of course. His name was Isaackjee. He was very thin and small, with big, owl-like eyes. He always dressed in loose pyjamas and a shirt a size too large for him, and wore an enormous skullcap on his head. Everybody knew him and he knew everybody. Isaackjee was like a walking, talking encyclopedia of the Jewish community. He knew all the Jewish families of Alibaug, our family names, our village names, meaning our kars, our problems. He was the perfect source for juicy gossip about our people. For each family he had fixed timings. When he came to our homes with a message, he was served cold drinks and snacks. Some people offered him food and even packed some for his family. To add to this, for every message he delivered, he received a tip.'

'What happened to him?'

'He made an aliyah to Israel.'

'Do you remember how much he was paid for his job as a shamash?'

'Hardly anything. Both the shamash and the hazzan were paid very little for their services, but lived on charity. The community looked after them. I am sure it was hard to survive on that sort of salary, as Isaackjee had nine children! His wife supplemented their income by making snacks for Jewish families. She took orders to make Kippur chi puri for the Day of Atonement and chik cha halwa for the New Year. With her daughter-in-law's help, she continues to do the same in Israel.'

'What about Isaackjee?'

'He died a few years ago.'

'Do you think I could meet Hassaji Daniyal?'

'Yes, on your way back, before you go to the harbour, just go to the Alibaug beach and ask for him. But why do you want to meet him?'

'I just want to ask him some questions, as I am sure he knows how the committee functions and how they allotted work among themselves.'

'You can try. But he is a very bitter man.'

'Why?'

'It is natural.'

Judah sat deep in thought for several moments. 'Did he always have a horse?' he asked eventually.

'Yes, all of us had a horse carriage or a bullock cart. He always came in his horse carriage to conduct the services. But as a cantor he earned so little that he could not support his wife and children. That is the time he decided to make good use of his horse. He started hiring out his carriage for some time, but since people started using autorickshaws, nobody wanted a horse carriage. Since then, he had no use for either horse or carriage. He was planning to sell the horse, but I advised him against it and suggested that he make good use of it by giving joy rides to children. I bought all that he needed to make the horse look attractive, a new saddle, blinkers and some fancy trappings. It worked. Now he earns enough to keep body and soul together.

But he is bitter, and if you ever meet him on Friday evening at the Alibaug synagogue, he will tell you his story. Sometimes he conducts the Sabbath services there, if and when there is a minyan of ten men or a group of Jews from abroad.'

'Is he secretive, or will he talk?'

'You can tell him you are my guest and a friend of Jacob's. But what would you gain by meeting him?'

'Public opinion!' Judah laughed.

'Ah, that,' said Rachel, 'was Prophet Elijah's idea.'

'The Prophet? When did you last have a conversation with him?'

'Do you remember that night when I came to your house? You had not said anything about public opinion, yet I thought you had. The term kept playing in my mind. I am sure now that it was the Prophet who planted the word in my mind on my way back in the catamaran.' She paused, touched her fingers to her eyes and asked, 'But tell me, what are your plans?'

'First I will speak to Hassaji Daniyal. Then I will look for some Jewish elders from Bombay who may want to support us.'

'I thought you said you did not like to mix with the community?'

'The Prophet Elijah told me that I should,' he laughed. 'In the meantime Aunty, do speak to your family in Israel and ask them to help us. But before that, I must meet hazzanbaba.'

'If you are planning to meet him today, take something for him.'

'Like what?'

'Besan laddoos!'

METHI BHAAJI

Ingredients: methi or fenugreek leaves, potatoes, onions, garlic, oil, red chilli powder, coconut, salt

Method: Take two fresh bouquets of methi, cut root ends, pluck leaves, wash well and soak in a large bowl of water, changing water frequently to get rid of residue. When washed clean, drain methi leaves and keep aside.

Slice three onions, chop six cloves garlic and fry till golden brown in two tablespoons oil. Add one large potato peeled and cubed. When potato is almost done, mix well with methi leaves, chilli powder and salt. Cover the pan and cook on slow fire in its own liquid till cooked. Add a heaped tablespoon of freshly grated coconut.

Methi is a bitter herb and coconut helps reduce the bitterness.

Cook on slow fire, till the vegetable absorbs the oil. Serve hot with chapattis.

Optional: Use jaggery instead of grated coconut.

Variation: Vegetables like gavar or cluster beans, french beans, snake gourd, dudhi or marrow, tindla and padval can be cooked in the same way.

A sprig of fenugreek is used as karpas or the bitter herb in the Pessach platter if parsley is not available.

Methi has medicinal values and is known to cure constipation. A plain bitter soup made with methi leaves is supposed to have medicinal value when taken early in the morning on an empty stomach. A few methi seeds, soaked and swallowed whole, are also known to cure many ailments.

Whenever Rachel made methi, she missed Jacob. He loved methi and when he was in India he lived on it. Rachel called him methi-mad. And, just for him, she had a patch of methi growing in her backyard. Rachel never understood how Jacob had developed a taste for this bitter herb, which was disliked by the rest of the family. She wondered whether it had anything to do with his thumb-sucking habit as a child.

Soon after Rachel had weaned Jacob from her breast to the milk bottle, he had taken to sucking his thumb. This continued and Rachel was worried when he was four years old and still sucking his thumb. She was ashamed. His habit made her miserable, especially when they went to the synagogue. For no reason at all she felt all eyes were on Jacob. Even if they did not say anything, she felt the women were laughing at her. Rachel would nudge Jacob, whisper veiled threats, scold him and even bandage his hand. Jacob would sulk as they walked to the synagogue, watching his mother with big watery eyes, ready to burst into tears.

Jacob would sit next to his mother in the synagogue, hiding his bandaged hand in the folds of her sari. He felt insulted but suffered till he could bear it no longer. The prayers were long and his mother kept her eyes averted. Besides, she had not hugged him even once. The sobs collected in his chest and he needed his thumb.

Rachel smiled as she remembered that once during a particular lull in the prayers Jacob had let out a wail so loud and long that the men looked up at the women's gallery. Aaron also looked up at Rachel, his brow darkened with anger that a child of his was making a scene at the synagogue.

The women collected around Jacob and made every possible effort to soothe him, but he would not stop crying because his mother sat next to him, still as a statue, ignoring him. It was then that Rubybai, sitting next to Rachel, saw the bandaged hand. Rachel had often told her how perturbed she was about Jacob's thumb-sucking habit. Squatting on the floor, she held Jacob in her arms and asked Rachel if she could take off the bandage, as the child was suffering.

Cornered and annoyed, Rachel watched them doting over Jacob, feeling both resentment and anger, caught in a web of conflicting emotions. When Rubybai removed the bandage from his hand, Jacob's tears turned into smiles and he quickly started sucking his thumb. Snuggled up in Rubybai's sumptuous lap, he fell asleep with an expression of bliss.

As the men continued with the prayers, the women whispered and discussed the problem of thumb-sucking among older children. Rachel felt humiliated that she had not been able to handle such a small matter. She was in tears as the women gave her some age-old remedies to cure Jacob. Rachel returned home wiser and decided upon a mixture of castor oil and fenugreek powder.

The next morning, after Jacob had had his milk bottle and was about to fall asleep with thumb in mouth, she applied a layer of the mixture on his thumb. He threw up and watched his thumb suspiciously, pursed his lips, sucked the air and was not sure whether he liked it or not. Much to Rachel's surprise, he did not suck his thumb, but played with it for a couple of hours, then fell asleep, watching his hand.

Since then, the bitter herb was like a bond between mother and son. So much so that whenever Rachel made methi, Jacob invariably phoned her. Rachel wondered, now how did he know?

On one such afternoon, after a lunch of leftover roast meat from the night before, methi and chapattis, Rachel was dozing on the veranda when the phone rang. Instinctively, she knew it was Jacob.

'How did you know it was me?'

'I knew. Did you make methi for lunch?'

'Yes Mama. I called to say that today I found methi in the Indian shop in Beersheba.'

'Fresh?'

'No, dry and packed.'

'I am glad. Tell Ilana to soak it well in water, drain and cook with lots of onion and coconut.'

'I will. But what are you doing right now?'

'Worrying.'

'About what?'

'The synagogue.'

'What are you planning to do?'

'Ah!' she laughed, 'I am trying to create public opinion.'

'How?'

'That is the problem.'

'Is Judah of any help at all?'

'Why do you ask?'

'Because I know he is stubborn. He takes up cases only if they interest him. What does he have to say?'

'Judah is doing everything possible to help me.'

'At last, somebody appreciates him.'

'What do you mean?'

'I was one of the few close friends he had. Others thought he was rude and abrupt.'

'He is, but we get along very well. He is very helpful.'

'Yes, Zephra told me.'

'What did she tell you?'

'She told me how you have become an activist. We are trying to help you.'

'How?'

'I have contacted the Indian association of Jews here and we are going to start a signature campaign.'

'How will that help?'

'A campaign like that is the beginning of public opinion. In this way, Jews abroad know what is happening to our synagogue. As a beginning, the committee of the synagogue in Danda will receive a letter from us, after which they will realize that they cannot take such decisions on their own.'

'Then?'

'Once we get all the details, Aviv will start collecting donations.'

'Aviv?' Rachel asked in surprise.

'Yes, he has already sent a circular to the members of the Indian association in Israel.'

'I thought he was always busy, very busy.'

'Aviv is making a list of possible donors.'

'What will I do with the money?'

'If you want to save the synagogue, you need money.'

'I am not good at organizing anything.'

'You are—look how you have roped in Judah.'

'We get along very well.'

'That is a miracle, because he has always maintained a distance from the Jewish community. He must be really fond of you.'

'Yes, I think he is, and I am fond of him.'

'Perhaps I should speak to him about the signature campaign.'

'Do you have his phone number?'

Rachel gave him Judah's phone number, went back to her chair and fell into a reverie about the family. Feeling sad and alone, she decided to take a stroll around the synagogue.

She changed her sari, powdered her face, covered her head and took the shortest route to the synagogue. She kissed the mezuzah, opened the lock and saw a ray of light falling on the teva from the broken stained-glass window upstairs. Rachel thanked the Lord for the beauty he had bestowed upon her.

Soon there would be a guard at the door. He would have the power to stop her from entering the house of the Lord. She saw the grounds of the synagogue transform into flowerbeds like in a picture postcard: clean, neat and full of flowers with a fragrance of talcum powder. She detested the idea.

Rachel dusted the teva, the chairs and the benches. Then, leaving the door wide open, she filled a bucket of water from the garden tap and returned to see Mordecai standing there with an angry look on his face. He did not smile or greet her. Rachel also did not think it necessary to greet him, yet asked politely what had brought him there at such an unusual hour.

He looked at her sternly. 'Who is Judah Abraham?' 'What about him?'

'He is asking too many questions.'

'So what is wrong with asking questions?'

'There is nothing wrong with asking questions, but I believe you have employed him to hound us.'

'What do you mean?' Rachel asked, indignant.

'You know very well what I am saying.'

'If you have come here to pick a fight, you are knocking at the wrong door.'

'You know, I could stop you from entering the synagogue.'

Rachel looked at him defiantly. 'Try,' she said, dangling the bunch of the synagogue keys under his nose.

Mordecai had not expected her to react like this. He had assumed she would cow down and beg his forgiveness for having asked Judah Abraham to meddle in the affairs of the synagogue. In a flash, Mordecai changed his tone and said, 'Come on sister, I was just joking.'

Rachel was adamant. 'Using such language with me is no joke.'

'Sister Rachel, why are you so angry? At least you could offer me a cup of tea.'

'Brother Mordecai, don't you know that there is no tea in the house of the Lord?'

'All right, so why don't you invite me to your house?'

'As usual, if you had come to my house, instead of the synagogue, perhaps I could have offered you something as flatulent as peethal.'

'Sorry for the mistake. I have been so upset about this Judah Abraham of yours that I did not know what to do. As soon as I arrived, I went to your house. The door was locked. So I assumed you were here.'

Hiding her resentment, Rachel told him to wait on the veranda of her house. She locked the synagogue, returned to the house and saw Mordecai sitting regally on her deckchair. 'How dare he sit on my chair,' she mumbled to herself and hastened to make tea for her unwelcome guest.

With cups of tea and a plate of biscuits between them, Rachel relaxed. Mordecai said he resented that an unknown Jewish gentleman with the name of Judah Abraham had had a long conversation with the old cantor, Hassaji Daniyal.

Placing the cup back on the table, he said rather reproachfully, 'We have known each other for such a long time. You could have at least phoned me and I would have answered all your questions. Why did you have to ask this Judah to investigate into the committee's decision to lease the land around the synagogue?'

'Judah is not a stranger—he is like my son.'

'He may be, but we do not know him.'

'What do you mean, you do not know him? He belongs to our community.'

'I do not deny that, but has he ever mixed with us?'

'That is his personal matter. None of your business.'

'Yet, he is more of an outsider than insider.'

'You mean, if a person does not step into a synagogue or does not attend a malida, you can state that he does not belong to the Jewish community? I do not accept that.'

'Since when have you become so modern?'

'I have always been modern.'

'So tell me, what is the meaning of being a Jew, if this Judah has never attended a single prayer at the synagogue?'

'These are matters of the heart. There is no logic to a question like that.'

'How can you say that? Do you know this Judah?'

'I repeat again, he is not "this Judah". He is a very nice young man at heart—he is as much a Jew as you and me.'

'How can you be so sure of that?'

'Because I am not a bad judge of character. He is as concerned about the synagogue as I am.'

'What about the synagogue?' Hawk-eyed Mordecai was watching her.

Rachel sat upright and said, 'You know what I am talking about.'

'Are you referring to Mr Chinoy's visit to the synagogue?'

'Yes. I have understood that you want to sell the synagogue.'

'No, you haven't understood anything.'

'I understood very well.'

'Let me explain. You know very well that we have no money to run the synagogue. The community is fast disappearing. Everybody has left for Israel, even your children. Where is the minyan of ten men to hold the Sabbath services? So we decided to lease out the land around the synagogue for a couple of years. Then we would know what to do with the synagogue.'

'That is if you and I are alive to see that day. By then, Mr Chinoy will see to it that the land becomes his property and the synagogue will disappear from the face of the earth.'

'He is not that sort of man.'

'Just wait and see.'

'But why are you interfering and sending this Judah after us? We, the elders of the committee, know what we are doing.'

'Judah is a well-known lawyer and he is helping me to save the synagogue.'

'How do you come into the picture?'

'Because I look after the synagogue and belong to the Bene Israel community of this land.'

Mordecai sat up defiantly in Rachel's chair and said, 'As far as we are concerned, you are just the caretaker of the synagogue.' Saying that, he rose to his feet and walked out of the house without looking back.

Smarting from the insult, Rachel stood shivering, angry and not knowing what to do. Suddenly she felt something like a roar rise within her. 'Stop!' she ordered.

Mordecai looked back, surprised, and his bag fell from his hand. As he bent to pick it up, he saw her towering over him, hands on waist, brow furrowed.

'So, I am merely the caretaker, sort of a servant, that you can throw me out as though I am the sweeper woman? No, you cannot. You seem to have forgotten that I am Rachel Dandekar. I belong to an illustrious family. Do you remember names like Abraham, Solomon, Menashe, Enoch, Joseph and Joshua, my ancestors? I will not allow you to treat me like a common labourer. Just wait, you Mordecai, I will make you eat your words.' Then opening the wicket gate, she ordered him out, saying, 'Don't you dare enter my house ever again.'

CHAY

Ingredients: tea, water, sugar, milk

Method: For two cups of tea, you need one and half cups of water and half cup milk, one teaspoon of your favourite tea, stronger the better, and three teaspoons of sugar.

Boil water, add sugar, boil for a minute, add tea and brew till rich brown in colour. Add milk and boil till it turns milky brown. Cover and let the tea stand for a minute or two, before pouring into cups. If you wish to add cardamom, mint or ginger to your tea, they should be added with the sugar.

Hot tea, served with piping hot bhajjis, is a popular combination for rainy days.

Optional: Tea is often made with cardamom or fresh mint, lili chay and a small piece of crushed ginger.

❧

According to Jewish dietary law, vessels used to make tea must be kept separately, so that the flavour of tea remains pure.

Rachel tried to keep herself busy. But her thoughts kept going back to Mordecai's insults. Just because she was alone, the committee had assumed that she was at their mercy. Her dedication to the synagogue had gone to waste.

She felt angry and disturbed that Aviv, Jacob and Zephra were so far away. Rachel saw their photographs on the mantelpiece and put the frames face downwards. She wanted to be with them. She had always believed that a family had to eat together to stick together. Perhaps she too should have left with them for Israel. But she was not comfortable with the idea of changing her dress or living a life that was not familiar. Yet, if people like Mordecai were going to treat her like a maidservant, she would have to pack her bags and leave.

Rachel picked up the phone to tell Aviv that at last she had decided to immigrate to Israel. He would not believe her, but yes, she would join them in Israel, even wear jeans and eat falafel, if necessary. At least she would not feel abandoned.

But nobody was at home, so haltingly she left a message on the answering machine. Then, with tears streaming down her face, Rachel phoned Judah and told him how Mordecai had insulted her. He promised to reach Danda as soon as possible. She felt better—he was there to protect her. Yet, she felt alone and lost.

Rachel looked out of the window and saw that dark clouds were collecting over the sea; perhaps there would be a heavy downpour. She felt depressed and lonely.

On days like these, she often went over to Kirtibai's house. She felt the beginning of a headache and took an aspirin, powdered her face to camouflage the tears and touched some eau de cologne on her throbbing temples, changed into a pale-blue sari and, passing a comb through her hair, told herself, I feel like a widow and a childless one at that.

Locking the door, Rachel walked over to Kirtibai's house with her umbrella. Kirtibai's house was bustling with women, children and grandchildren. She felt better. As the older women sat on the sofa and talked, the younger women ran in and out of the kitchen, serving them tea and snacks.

Kirtibai held Rachel's cold hand in hers. 'Tell me what is bothering you. Try as you may, you cannot possibly hide anything from me. You are laughing and joking with the children, but I can see that your eyes are sad.'

'Arre, what am I to say? I feel lonely with the family in Israel. Here, I have nobody of my own.'

'Why? What about us? We are your family, nako?'

Rachel looked out of the window. 'My children, they are so far away.'

'I understand, but you decided against Israel. This is an old story. It is not about Israel—something else is bothering you.'

When Rachel told Kirtibai the events of the last few days, she felt better. Outside, the crescendo of thunder and lightning rose. Rachel shivered. With umbrella in hand she prepared to leave and her face fell at the thought of spending the evening by herself.

Kirtibai asked her to spend the day with them. Rachel was about to say yes when the fishmonger's son came looking for her, saying that she had a guest standing at her door. It was the tall young man with glasses, and, if she wanted to make dinner for him, he had a big, fat pomfret for her.

'Judah,' Rachel whispered and, rejecting the fish, prepared to leave.

Kirtibai was all smiles. 'Ah, your spiritual son has arrived. He cannot possibly leave you alone in times like these. Your deva heard your prayers. He is there to protect you.' She then called out to her daughters-in-law, asking her to pack some bhajjis and patrel for her. Rachel took the box of food, gave Kirtibai a tight hug and opened her enormous black umbrella. She rushed down the steps, jumped over the slush and ran towards her house, with Kirtibai calling out to her, 'Slowly, slowly, halu, halu, be careful, don't break your leg.'

Rachel waved and disappeared around the bend which led to her house.

She was panting when she reached the house, happy to see Judah standing on the veranda filling the cup of his hands with rainwater, just like Aviv.

Closing the umbrella and wiping her face, Rachel stood shivering. Judah walked up to her and hugged her as the tears ran down her cheeks. He helped her into a chair and offered her a glass of water. Then he went into the kitchen, saying, 'I will first make you some tea. We need something to cool our nerves.'

Judah returned with two cups and asked if she had biscuits in the house.

'Are you hungry?' asked Rachel.

'Yes.'

'I am in no mood to cook, but I have chapattis and Kirtibai gave me these bhajjis and patrel. They are good with tea. Have some. And, now that you are here, I will make a vegetable.'

'What?'

'Something easy and quick, say, karelas. They will kill the bitterness within me.'

'Perfect.'

FISH ALBERAS

Ingredients: pomfret, oil, garlic, onion, ginger, green chillies, potato, coconut, coriander leaves, mint, curry leaves, tomato, cumin, turmeric, cocum, salt

Method: Take a big pomfret, remove teeth, leave eyes, chop tail ends, cut into six or seven pieces, salt and keep aside.

Prepare masala with six cloves garlic, half inch piece of ginger, a bouquet of fresh coriander, a few leaves fresh mint, two green chillies and one tomato. Grind or pass masala through a mixer with very little water.

Make coconut milk with a freshly grated coconut or use tinned coconut milk.

Heat two tablespoons oil in a casserole and splutter a few curry leaves. Fry one finely chopped onion till transparent, add the masala, cook on a slow fire till masala absorbs oil. Add one cup coconut milk with half cup water, a pinch turmeric and half teaspoon cumin powder. Add fish with one potato, peeled and cut into six pieces, cook on slow fire. When done, add four leaves of wet cocum or mangosteen and

cook on slow fire till gravy thickens and has a fresh
green colour.
Serve hot with coconut rice.
Optional: This recipe is also made with red chilli
powder and a squeeze of lemon instead of green
chillies and cocum.

❧❧

Aviv called, livid that Mordecai had insulted his mother. He
was now on the warpath and speaking to the leaders of the
Indian community in Israel.

Rachel felt better. She was sure Zephra would also call, but
she did not. She wanted to speak to her daughter. The next day,
she even called her kibbutz and somebody answered in Hebrew.
The barrier of tongues annoyed Rachel.

It was two days before Zephra called. At midnight. Happy to
hear her voice, Rachel started telling her about Mordecai. Zephra
comforted her. 'Hold on Mama, we can speak when I reach home.'

'What do you mean?'

'I am very close to you.'

'How? You are in Israel, nako?'

'No, I am not.'

'Then where are you?'

'Guess.'

'I cannot.'

'All right, you will not believe this, but I am at Bombay airport.'

Rachel gasped, and in a voice choked with emotion all Zephra
could say was, 'I am staying here till dawn. Then I will take a
taxi to Gateway and reach home as soon as I find the first
catamaran.'

That night Rachel could not sleep. Turning restlessly in bed,
she thought of the days when Zephra was a little girl. She wanted
to be at the door when Zephra arrived. Yet, without wanting to,
she fell asleep. It was Zephra who woke her up by calling out
and rattling the gate.

Mother and daughter embraced and Rachel whispered, 'Just like you, always full of surprises.'

Rachel studied her daughter, dressed as always in her trademark blue jeans and white tee shirt. Her hair was shorter and she appeared taller, plumper and more beautiful than ever.

Rachel washed her face, brushed her teeth and worried that she did not have coffee for Zephra. There was some in a bottle, but when she opened it, she saw that it had crystallized into a little brown rock. Sensing her mother's unease, Zephra told her not to worry—she would have tea the way Rachel made it with crushed cardamoms. Rachel looked into the plastic bag Zephra had given her on the way to her room and saw that she had remembered to pick up bread and butter from the Alibaug bakery.

Mother and daughter sat on the veranda with their tea cups, as Zephra regaled Rachel with stories of her last-minute dash to India and how Aviv had rushed to the airport, just to give her a glass cleaner, the one their mother liked, with the lavender fragrance.

Rachel smiled happily and went to the kitchen to make a breakfast of fried eggs and toast. Zephra ate well, then had a shower and changed into a frayed, old white Punjabi suit. It was her old school uniform. Whenever she was in India, Zephra used it as a nightdress. She sat listening to Rachel's problems. Halfway through her tale, Rachel noticed that Zephra was dozing in her chair. She led her daughter to the bed and tucked her in, as though she were a little girl.

Zephra woke up to the fragrance of her mother's famous green masala curry. The house felt warm, as if she were sleeping under a quilt on a winter morning. She loved fish albless, or was it pronounced alberas? She was never sure. Strange how she had tried to remember the name of the recipe in Israel. Try as she may, she could never get the name right, but, lying soaked in its flavour, the name came back to her.

Then she heard voices. There was somebody else in the house. They were talking softly. She was annoyed to hear a man's voice in the house. On her first night in India, she wanted to be alone with her mother. Zephra was in no mood to meet friends or relatives.

She could not recognize the voice and told herself that, if he was in their house at this hour, he had to be an enemy.

She got out of bed and switched on the light and made sure that she was decently dressed, the way her mother liked her to look, covered from neck to heel. It had taken Rachel a couple of years to get adjusted to seeing Zephra in shorts. To please her mother, she even threw a dupatta around her shoulders.

Zephra emerged from her room, puffy eyed and still groggy from sleep. She was surprised to see Rachel sitting cross-legged on her deckchair, deep in discussion with a young man she did not recognize.

Rachel sensed her presence. 'Come,' she said, 'meet Judah, my lawyer.'

They shook hands. Rachel knew from past experience that Zephra was in no mood to meet Judah so she behaved as though his presence in the house was the most natural thing on earth, saying, 'Do you remember Judah, a friend of Jacob's?'

He stood up politely, offering Zephra a chair and greeting her with a casual 'shalom'. She returned his greeting, but did not accept the chair, instead stood where she was, leaning against the doorpost and watching him curiously.

Feeling uncomfortable and sensing her resentment, he explained rather hastily, 'Had I known you were coming, I would not have dropped in. Even Aunty did not call me and inform me of your arrival. She must have been too excited to remember that I often take a catamaran in the evenings to meet her.'

When Zephra did not answer he continued, 'I understand, tonight you would like to be alone with your mother. I will return to Alibaug as soon as I have discussed some urgent matters with her.'

Touched by his concern for her mother, Zephra accepted the chair he offered her. 'Do you think she will allow you to return to Bombay without tasting her famous fish alberas?' she sighed. 'And I will have to share it with you. I am sure you know that she has specially made it for me.'

Judah gave her a guarded half smile. 'As a rule, I stay back for dinner and return the next morning. Any objections?'

'Why should I? You really make me sound like a devil.'

'Well, I am scared of you. If I remember correctly, as a kid you almost scratched my eyes out when I refused an extra helping of rice.'

'I always thought you were rude and stubborn.'

'I still am.'

'You know, I had given you a nickname. Want to know?'

'Yes,' he smiled.

'Green-eyed Monster.'

When Rachel set the table, she was relieved that the two young people were laughing. She had dreaded their meeting. The light banter continued to the dining table, as Zephra took large helpings of the curry in a bowl and drank it like a soup. Rachel laughed. Judah watched her as he had never heard her laugh since they met.

He did not know that, secretly, Rachel was happy, because at last Zephra was showing some interest in this young man from Bombay. Rachel was already matchmaking. She liked the idea of them as a couple. But, as a mother, she also knew that she could not possibly interfere in Zephra's life. If Zephra ever sensed that her mother was scheming she would resent it.

Rachel looked at the sky and left it to the Lord to arrange this particular marriage in heaven. It was He who had sent the groom, it was for Him to convince the bride. That is, if she was willing to accept this divine proposal.

Rachel had to control herself to not show too much interest in them. So she busied herself between the kitchen and the dining room, doing this and that and leaving them alone, hoping they would take a liking to each other.

That night, Rachel slept peacefully, as the house was fragrant with the breath of her beautiful daughter.

The next day, Rachel and Judah explained to Zephra the problems about the synagogue. She had come from Israel to Danda, driven more by emotion than reason. Not sure of her role in the picture, she asked her mother, 'Mama, what have you done with all that money?'

Rachel gave her a blank look. 'Which money? I have no money.'

Zephra stood up, put her arms around her mother's shoulders and, rubbing her cheek to her mother's, murmured, 'My dear, forgetful Mama.'

Watching Zephra's bronzed cheeks glowing, Judah had goose pimples and he had a great desire to touch her. Her husky cigarette voice disturbed him. For years, no woman had stirred him as much as Zephra. He looked away, afraid that she would read his thoughts. They were just building a bond of friendship and he did not want anything to spoil that. It was also very important that one of Rachel's family members be present in Danda while she was fighting for the synagogue.

Judah had always kept a distance from women, especially Jewish women, though he could not deny that he had been in love with his law-school friend Sujata. He closed his eyes with the memory of her round face and emerald-green eyes. Actually, that is what had attracted them to each other. It had been so many years ago that Judah could not even remember what had actually drawn them close and eventually thrown them far apart.

A voice cut through his reverie. He opened his eyes and was staring into Zephra's dark eyes, dark as the sea at midnight. She was smiling. 'You were somewhere else. Look, we have just discovered that my mother is a rich woman.'

'How come?' he asked, sitting up and making sure his eyes did not betray him.

'Very simple. For years, the family and others have been sending Mama some money for herself and the synagogue. And, like a good Jew, she has been putting it away in the bank and that is how she has enough and more money to spend on the synagogue or even buy it, if necessary.'

Rachel giggled like a child. 'I really believed that I had a meagre bank balance and no funds at all to fight the committee. I am glad Zephra asked me about it and we checked the balance. The last time he was here, Mordecai made me feel like a beggar,' her voice choked, 'as though I was at his mercy, a paid servant.' The giggles turned to sobs and Zephra held her mother and let her cry, as Judah busied himself in the kitchen. Zephra looked around to see what he was doing there while she was comforting her mother. 'Strange fellow,' she murmured to herself. Rachel wiped her eyes, looked up and asked, 'Kay? What did you say?'

'Nothing,' said Zephra.

She knew how her mother's mind worked. Just one wrong word here and there would trigger off her matchmaking instincts.

Judah emerged from the kitchen with three cups of black tea. He had made it exactly the way Rachel liked it. She took a sip and felt better. Zephra smiled and complimented Judah, 'You make excellent tea.'

'Thank you. That is all I can make.'

'It is really good, see how Mama is smiling.'

'She had better smile, she is a rich woman.'

'How do I use the money?' said Rachel. 'I am so confused.'

'We have to make a plan,' Zephra said and, seeing Judah light a cigarette, borrowed one from him.

They sat smoking silently for a while; Judah was trying to remember something Rachel had told him. 'Aunty, do you remember the name of the wife of your friend Chinoy-Finoy?'

'She did tell me her name when she entered the house, but I don't remember, because she reminded me so much of Zephra. But that one was smart, not innocent like my Zephra. She saw I was lonely and tried to maska me, telling me, "Aunty will you teach me how to make bombils,"' she mimicked, 'as though I did not understand her game. I know the type. She had noticed that

I was resentful about the land deal. Mordecai had once brought this strange-looking flower to impress me. I was so angry and told him exactly what I thought of him. To me it looked more like a spider than a flower.'

Zephra was amused. 'Mama, that is funny, but try to remember her name?'

'What name?'

'Oh, Mama, don't be difficult. The name of Chinoy's wife.'

'Mrs Chinoy.'

'Mama, you are being naughty. I know you never forget names. Look how you tracked down Judah.'

'That is different—I needed him.'

'So, perhaps you may also need this Mrs Chinoy. You cannot deny that she was kind.'

'That she was.'

'And you also melted when she said, "Aunty will you teach me how to make bombils." If her wretched husband was not around, I know, you would have cooked bombils for her, fed her, packed some for her to take home and even given her the recipe in your fancy Marathi handwriting.'

'I did not, because I thought she was trying to maska me.'

Judah laughed. 'So, tell us her name.'

Rachel changed the subject. 'I like your laugh, you should laugh more often.'

'You too, but before we start laughing and forget everything, do tell us her name.'

As Zephra and Judah bent towards her, she whispered, 'Kay . . . she had a nice name like Kavita or something like that. Her husband called her by that name. He was in a hurry, but she had stopped to talk to me.'

Zephra sat up. 'Kavita what?'

'Chinoy, what else?'

'No, no, I mean what is her maiden name?'

'How do you expect me to know such details? This woman turns up at my door with her husband and you do not expect me to ask her maiden name. Anyway, Mordecai was doing all the talking, while her husband was watching everybody from behind his dark glasses, but not missing a word. He was listening attentively to all that was being said. Poor woman, she could hardly get a word in. Had I spent a little more time with her, I could have asked her more about herself. I admit she seemed to have a kind heart.'

'Can you describe her to me?' asked Zephra thoughtfully.

'She was of medium height and build, almost like you. Long face, very fair, large grey eyes and had an enormous mole on her chin.'

'You know Mama, I think I know her.'

'How?'

'Because she cannot be anybody else but Kavita Shahni who used to be with me in college.'

'So, you know her?'

'Yes.'

'How can you be so sure that she is the same Kavita?'

'Because there cannot be any other Kavita with grey eyes and a mole on the chin.'

'Even if you know her, how does it make a difference?'

'That makes a lot of difference—we can at least speak to her.'

'About what?'

'About her husband.'

'What about her husband?'

'We will try to explain to her about the synagogue.'

'How will that help?'

'She will understand and try to help us.'

'I don't think she has a voice,' said Rachel, dismissing the subject.

Zephra smiled. 'My dear mother, I suppose you know that women have ways and means of getting around their men. Do you remember how you used to get around Papa? There were times when he was stubborn and impossible, but somehow you always managed to convince him.'

'That,' agreed Rachel, 'is true.'

'So, let us meet Kavita,' said Zephra. 'I cannot believe that she is Mrs Chinoy. She used to be pretty, but very affectionate. If I am right, she is the same girl. In fact, I remember that we took lunch boxes to college as it was expensive to eat out every day. We were a group of six and shared the food. And I also remember that Kavita ate all the bombils while I feasted on her parathas. If it is the same Kavita, I am sure she was not buttering you when she said she wanted to learn how to make bombils. She developed a taste for bombils because of me. Let us give her a chance, because she used to be simple and unassuming. I quite liked her. Wonder how she is doing as Mrs Chinoy?'

'From your description she does not sound like the same girl because this one was very smart.'

Judah said drily, 'Women change with marriage. The point is, how do we find her?'

Rachel made a face. 'I am sure Mordecai has Chinoy's phone number. But I do not want to speak to him.'

'You said they have a farmhouse in Alibaug,' said Zephra.

'Yes!'

'All we have to do is find the number from directory inquiry and phone her,' said Zephra, picking up the phone.

Her mother stopped her and said, 'Don't worry, I have the number. She had given me this fancy card of hers and as usual I shoved it under the telephone.' Rachel put on her spectacles, picked up the instrument, found the card and gave it to Zephra.

Kavita was not in Alibaug, but the caretaker gave her a Bombay number, where she was told Kavitamemsaab was not at home. But she could leave her number and Madam would call back.

The next morning, Zephra woke up at the insistent ringing of the telephone. Rachel was in the courtyard feeding the birds and there was no sign of Judah. It was Kavita at the other end, excited that Zephra had called after all these years. She wanted to know if she was on holiday in India and if the entire family had moved to Israel.

Zephra informed her that her mother still lived in Danda. 'Do you remember how you used to love those bombils in my lunch box?' she reminded her. 'Mama used to make them.'

'Yes, I haven't eaten such bombils since our college days.'

'Yes, my mother is a great cook. By the way, a month or so ago, you met her.'

'Met your mother? How is that?'

'You did. I suppose you came with your husband to see the land around our house, near the synagogue in Danda.'

'Ah, yes, Aunty Rachel. My husband's friend who had taken us there told me that she was famous for her cooking.'

Zephra cursed under her breath. 'Are you talking about Uncle Mordecai?'

'Yes. What a surprise! I did not know that Aunty Rachel was your mother. I had also forgotten that you used to come to college all the way from Alibaug.'

'I am so glad you met my mother.'

'I had accompanied my husband on a business trip. Normally on such occasions I never get involved. I am a pucca housewife. You know we have a house in Alibaug, we grow flowers and have a couple of beach resorts there. I did not know your mother still lives in Alibaug or I would have definitely visited her often.'

Zephra's voice became low. 'Yes, she decided to stay on here.'

'She does not like Israel?'

'No, she just does not want to leave Danda. She has a mission in life—looking after our synagogue.'

'Yes, I remember when they started talking about the synagogue, her face became stern and she was trying hard to be nice. I also saw that she would have liked to speak to me, but she hesitated, thinking I would only take advantage of her.'

'In a way that is true. I believe you wanted to know how to make bombils? She would have made them for you, but she was so angry . . .'

'I know she was very upset.'

'But, then, that is how I tracked you down. She described you and told me about your conversation and I knew it had to be you. Actually Kavita, we need your help.'

'Sure, but we must meet.' 'Are you coming to Alibaug?'

'Yes, in three days.'

'That is a Tuesday, so tell me, where shall we meet?'

'Let us have lunch at my place. I can ask the cook to make your favourite aloo parathas with raita.'

'I would love to come, but I want to spend time with Mama. So why don't you come to our place? You have seen the house. Mama will make bombils for you and, if you come early, you can also have a live cookery demonstration.'

'I am looking forward to that. I will be there before twelve.'

'Ciao.'

Zephra turned round to tell Judah all about the conversation and, not seeing him there, she called out to Rachel, 'Where the hell is your green-eyed monster? When you need him, he is never there. Has he gone back to Bombay or what?'

Rachel smiled.

SAAT PADAR

Ingredients: rice flour, coconut, sugar, wheat flour, cardamom, oil, eggs, salt and saffron

Method: Take two cups rice flour, half cup wheat flour, half cup sugar, a pinch salt and mix in a bowl. Make a thick batter with one cup coconut milk. Beat four eggs and gently fold into the mixture.

Add a few crushed cardamom seeds and a few strands of saffron or edible colour.

Heat oil in a frying pan and pour a tablespoon of the batter, spreading it evenly in the pan and forming a thin rice pancake.

When done on both sides, remove from pan and place on absorbent paper.

Fry the rest of the pancakes and keep aside. Place seven pancakes one on top of another, roll together like a scroll, cut into bite-size pieces and serve.

❦

Saat padar literally means 'the seven veils'.

Kavita and Zephra hugged each other warmly. They were meeting again after almost ten years. Unlike at their first meeting, Rachel hugged Kavita and welcomed her into the kitchen with a wide smile.

Kavita tied her hair in a clip and tucked her pallav around her waist, as Rachel showed her how to fry a bombil. Zephra was amused to see them frying bombils and talking in Marathi as if they had known each other for years. When lunch was ready, Rachel wanted to be left alone to give final touches to the pancakes, and the two young women caught up with news about old friends.

After lunch, they moved to the veranda, where Rachel settled in her deckchair. The younger women left her alone to doze and walked on the beach.

Zephra explained her mother's predicament to Kavita, whose face fell. Studying her drawn face, Zephra felt concerned and asked, 'Are you happy?'

Kavita gave a wry smile and said, 'Not that I am unhappy. Let me be honest with you. We, the daughters-in-law of the Chinoy family, do not have a voice. It was understood from the very beginning that we are not to interfere in the family business. But we are partners in business in a way, and we do sign all those blank cheques as we are part of the financial arrangement, but nothing more. Unfortunately I never know what is happening, nor am I told. If I ask, I am told that the women of the Chinoy family are supposed to manage all these houses we have and fulfil our social obligations.'

'So, how do you spend your time?'

'Actually I am very busy and have no time for myself. I plan lunches, dinner parties and make sure that all these houses run on oiled wheels. As Mrs Chinoy, I also inaugurate exhibitions or am present at women's meets. I go to the beauty parlour and the gym to keep trim as the smart bahu of the Chinoys. I also work with a local NGO.' She laughed. 'It's not that bad because I also have my happy moments. Twice a year we go on a holiday, one in India, the other abroad. That is when I spend time with my husband, as he does not have business lunches or meetings. Then I go to museums or the usual shopping sprees for clothes, perfumes and artefacts for our homes and offices.'

'Do you have children?'

'I have a son, Vikram. He is ten and in boarding school. When he is home for vacations is the time that I am really happy.'

'Kavita, I do not understand. If you are not part of your husband's business, how come you were there when he visited mother?'

'That morning, I wasn't planning to do anything. After breakfast, I was puttering around the house when Satish asked me if I would accompany him to meet a stubborn old lady for some land deal or the other. I did not know he was talking about Aunty Rachel, your mother. He said he was planning health resorts all along the seashore. I hate business meetings, but agreed half-heartedly.'

'Mama was right—she told me they had brought you along just to get around her.'

'I am ashamed to admit, but Aunty Rachel is right. In fact, she was trying hard to be rude. But the moment I saw her, I was enchanted. I forgot about the role I was supposed to play, although I saw my husband was trying to catch my eye through his glares. I avoided him and, fascinated, I watched Aunty Rachel. She was so graceful, so clever. To start with, I admit I was bored, but when I saw the way she was handling the men, I was interested and wanted to know her better. I didn't pay much attention to the conversation, but I was upset when Uncle Mordecai started insulting her, and even more so as I could not stop him. I had half a mind to tell him that this was no way to speak to an elderly lady, but had to keep my silence, as I knew my husband would cut me down right there in her presence. Instead, I tried to make a connection with Aunty Rachel by talking about bombils and all that. But, I must say, I am stupid.'

'Why do you say that?'

'When I entered your house, I saw your father's name plate, yet I did not guess that it was your house. And was Aunty Rachel stubborn! She did not allow anybody inside the house. She got rid of us from the veranda. If I had followed her into the drawing room, I would have seen your photograph on the mantelpiece and known it was your house.'

'That would have surprised your husband.'

'Yes, that would have complicated matters for him.'

'Kavita, tell me, do you think you can help us? Could you have some influence on your husband? We want to save the synagogue for Mama's sake.'

Kavita looked sad and dejected. 'Zephra, I may seem like a woman of power, but I cannot help you.'

'Mama also said that,' Zephra said quietly and Kavita smiled ruefully. 'Don't misunderstand me,' she said. 'I don't want to give you false promises.'

Zephra sat watching the sea and they were holding hands like in the good old days.

Kavita tried to change the subject. 'Now tell me something about yourself—are you married?'

Zephra's mood changed and she burst out laughing. 'No way. Do you see a wedding ring?'

'Nowadays, it is hard to tell whether a woman is married or not.'

'Why?'

'We have known each other for so long, and I feel you are wearing a mask. No, you don't look married, but surely you have a boyfriend?'

'Had.' A shadow of pain passed over Zephra's eyes. 'We were in the same kibbutz for five years. At first we were very good friends and then we fell in love. That was a mistake.'

'Why didn't you marry him? Five years is a long time.'

'I wanted to.'

'What happened?' 'Family pressure.'

'From which side?'

'Both.'

'I cannot believe it. Your family would be happy to see you married. Just this afternoon, Aunty tried to broach the subject at least five times, but you avoided it. You have become an expert at warding her off on that particular topic.'

'Actually she does not know about Zvi.' 'Why didn't you tell her?'

'She would have never understood. My brothers knew about him and we squabbled over him all the time.'

'Why?'

'They always maintained that they were protecting, not protesting. Because whenever they met Zvi, they were sure he was not serious about marriage.'

'Was it because he was white?'

'We do have a certain divide between the East European Jews, called Ashkenazi, and the Asian Sephardim Jews. We Indians are rather paranoid that Ashkenazi boys just play around with Asian women and are not serious about marriage. That's not exactly true, because Zvi would have married me, if he did not have his own doubts. What happened between us can happen to any two people, even if they are from the same community.'

'Is that what you meant when you said that both families objected?'

'At first, when he introduced me to his parents, they were very nice. But, at the end, he told me that they were pressurizing him not to marry me. This great divide may not be obvious, but it does come to the surface once in a while.'

'Zvi could not convince his parents?'

'He did not want to. Actually it was just an excuse. I think he had fallen out of love by then and was already seeing someone else.'

'Did that upset you very much?'

'In the beginning it did, but no longer. When we broke up, the first year was bad and I cried all the time. When I was not crying, I dated every possible boy on the kibbutz. But then I cooled down and now I am not seeing anybody. I haven't met anybody interesting,' Zephra sighed. 'Sometimes it gets rather lonely, but I do not want to make another mistake.' Then she smiled. 'Come, let's go back to the house. Mama must be wondering what's happened to us.'

Rachel was waiting for them, restless for her afternoon cup of tea and eager to know if Kavita would help them. Zephra went into the kitchen to make tea and Kavita sat next to Rachel, saying, 'Zephra has told me everything about the synagogue. Aunty, you are like family to me and I will tell you the truth. The situation in my house is such that I cannot help you.'

Rachel's face fell. Kavita said, 'Aunty you were right when you said I was just my husband's puppet. I cannot influence Satish in any way.' Kavita looked so helpless sitting at Rachel's knees that she held Kavita to her breast as though she were her own. When Zephra returned with the tea tray, she left it on the table and held them in the circle of her arms, saying, 'Don't worry. If we are together, we will find a way.'

They did not notice Judah, who had just returned from Bombay. He stood at the gate, not wanting to disturb them. For Judah, it was a victory of sorts. Instinctively, he knew that the woman in the yellow sari was Mrs Kavita Chinoy. This sentimental scene did not really move Judah and he could feel a devilish smile curve on his lips. Mrs Chinoy was exactly where he wanted her to be, on her knees. How he would make use of her was another matter.

Rachel looked up to see why Brownie was barking and why the cat had rushed to the gate. Why were the birds excited, and why was the goat bleating? Even before she saw him she knew Judah was standing at the gate, unsure whether he should enter the house or leave. But the animals and birds had created such a ruckus that he had no other alternative but to enter.

Embarrassed by his presence, the younger women disappeared into the house. Rachel stood alone on the veranda to greet him, and Judah gestured that it was better if he returned to Bombay.

Rachel wiped her face with her pallav, signalled that he should enter the house and poured him a cup of tea. Not knowing where to place himself, he sheepishly put down his briefcase and sat on the edge of a chair.

Zephra returned, eyes swollen and face flushed. Judah was watching her intently. He saw how vulnerable she was, as she smiled warmly and said, 'I must say, you are the original green-eyed monster. Turning up at all the unexpected moments. I really hate you.' Then, sensing that Kavita was standing next to her, she introduced her to Judah.

Apologetically, Judah drank the tea in one gulp, left the cup on the table, picked up his briefcase and made to leave. Zephra teased, 'I think, every evening, the fragrance of my mother's cooking wafts towards you in Bombay and you are drawn to faraway Danda. You know very well nothing pleases her more than that. And, as for mother, I am sure she has hidden your share of bombils in the meat safe, so how can you leave?'

Judah bowed dramatically, smiled, returned to his chair, pulled out a cigarette and offered it to her.

Kavita watched them, thinking they made a fine pair as they sat smoking and talking about the synagogue, much to Kavita's embarrassment. She was a trifle taken aback when Judah turned to her and asked, 'Mrs Chinoy, if you have a minute, I would like you to stay. I need your advice.'

'Kavita . . . Mrs Chinoy sounds too grand. Actually, I have explained everything to Zephra and Aunty Rachel. It is very difficult for me to say anything in the matter.'

'I guess so, but I just want to know your reactions about a plan I have in mind.'

Judah relaxed and sat cross-legged, hands placed over his knees in the stance of a professional lawyer. 'I suggest we use Aunty Rachel's secret fund, add some donations to it and make a museum, like the Joods museum in Amsterdam.'

Kavita relaxed. 'I was dreading to meet you, but what you say sounds good. Two years ago when we were in Amsterdam, I saw this Jewish museum you are talking about. It was a beautiful experience. If you plan something like that for Aunty's synagogue, I think I can help. But how I do not know.'

Together, they watched the evening light fall on the synagogue. Perhaps there was hope.

That night, with Judah on her right and Zephra on her left, Rachel lit a candle, asking the Prophet Elijah to help them protect the synagogue. Then, whispering to herself, she asked a personal favour, to help her with the matchmaking. After all, marriages are made in heaven, nako?

PURANPOLI

Ingredients: chana dal, refined flour, rice flour, wheat flour, sugar, a pinch nutmeg powder, cardamom, oil, vegetable ghee

Method: Soak overnight half a kilogram chana dal, wash and pressure cook with one cup water.

In another heavy-bottomed pan, mix the dal with the same amount of sugar and cook on slow fire, stirring continuously till the mixture becomes dry and paste- like in consistency. When cool, add a little powdered nutmeg and four crushed cardamom seeds and keep aside in another bowl.

Make dough with a quarter kilo each of the three types of flour with one cup water, or as required, and a tablespoon oil. Cover with cloth and let stand for more than an hour. The dough should have a soft consistency.

Make small ping-pong sized balls of dough, roll into small chapatti, place a tablespoon of dal filling in centre, bring edges together, pinch close and flatten down. Cover with rice flour and roll carefully into chapattis, roast on both sides on a thick griddle till done and spread half a teaspoon of vegetable ghee on the puranpoli. Serve hot.

Optional: If meat is not part of the meal, apply a layer of pure ghee or butter to the puranpoli and serve with a bowl of sweetened milk or a sour–sweet dal.

❦

Puranpoli is made on Purim in memory of the liberation of Persian Jews and the festival of Queen Esther. It falls on a full moon night with the Indian festival of colours, Holi, when mornings become warmer, but there is still a nip in the air, flowers blossom, and birds and animals mate. Purim heralds spring.

Rachel made puranpoli once a year for Purim. If she was alone she made two for herself, one for lunch and one for dinner, and more if she was with the family. She also made puranpoli whenever she was happy, say, for the birth of a grandchild or the homecoming of a child—or when she sensed that Zephra was attracted to Judah.

Zephra made several rounds to the kitchen, wondering why Rachel was making puranpoli. Rachel did not give herself away.

Zephra took one look at the ghee soaked puranpoli and made a face saying that she did not like sweets. She had lost weight with great difficulty and wanted to keep trim. Rachel smiled. 'Look at me, I eat more than all of you put together, but I haven't put on an ounce in thirty years. I am the same weight I was when I married your father.'

'Lucky you. Obviously I have taken after him. Remember how fat he was?'

'He loved my food and expected me to make different recipes every day. He had a good appetite and needed to take a walk after he had finished eating. He never did. Instead, soon after he ate, he would doze in his rocking chair. With the sea at the doorstep, he had the beach to himself and could have easily walked up and down, as many times as he wanted to, but never did. Remember, he would be fast asleep in the chair and one of us had to wake him up and help him to bed. Once his head touched the pillow, he would be snoring in five minutes flat.'

'That was later, but earlier was he fat or thin?'

'He was always a big-made man. Even as a boy, he was sort of fat. That is when we were teenagers and engaged to be married. I had already started preparations for the wedding, getting my trousseau ready and spending hours embroidering bed sheets and pillow covers with floral designs interwoven with words like good-luck and sweet-dreams. But, my dreams were short-lived. One afternoon, a year before the wedding, I was sitting on the veranda and embroidering a silk Sabbath tablecloth for my new home. I was so engrossed in my work that I did not hear the wicket gate rattle. My mother was sitting next to me, stitching a brocade border to a silk sari; softly she whispered, "Rachel, cover your legs, your mother-in-law is here."'

Rachel shuddered at the memory. 'I pulled my skirt over my ankles as she entered the house. I felt the premonition of danger. Her sudden visit and the look on her face spelt trouble. When I smiled, she did not smile back and looked agitated. So my mother sent me into the kitchen to make sherbet for her. While I was stirring the limbu paani in the kitchen, I heard the gate rattle and saw my mother-in-law walking out of the house, her shoulders slumped, her gait heavy. I did not know what was happening, so, leaving the glass where it was, I rushed out of the room to stop my mother-in-law. My mother caught hold of me, pulled me inside the house and closed the door. Her eyes were wet but she looked angry as she took my hand in hers and removed the engagement ring. I was hysterical and tried to snatch the ring away from her, but she held it in her fist, looking at me defiantly. It did not take me long to understand the meaning of her action—that my mother-in-law had just broken the engagement.'

Zephra gasped and reached out to comfort her mother. Rachel continued, 'My mother opened the tin truck in which she kept my wedding trousseau and put away the ring in the jewellery box. I felt helpless, watching her make neat packets of all that I had received as gifts from my in-laws. There were five silk saris with heavily embroidered borders, four blouses, eight pearl bangles, a diamond nose ring, silver anklets and a gold chain with a floral pendant. Packing everything in a tin trunk, she talked to herself, saying, according to tradition, we had to return all presents once an engagement was broken. Aaron's family would also return two pant pieces, a gold watch and the engagement ring.'

Rachel stopped, took a deep breath, drank a glass of water and went on, 'When my mother changed her sari and called for the bullock cart to take her to my in-laws' house to return the gifts, I stopped her. I wanted to know why my mother-in-law wanted to break the engagement. My mother snapped back, saying I was still a child and had no right to ask questions, but accept my fate. I had to accept the verdict of the elders without question. Because it was Aaron who wanted to break the engagement, for the simple reason that I was too thin for him. He had a preference for plump women like cousin Ronith; perhaps they were planning to send a manga for her. I was furious, how could Aaron fall in love with Ronith? Did my mother-in-law say that? I told my mother, if it was true, I would claw out Ronith's eyes. I had seen her making eyes at Aaron, during the engagement ceremony. She was teasing him far too much for my liking. These things were normal during celebrations, but she was going beyond all limits, making all those vulgar jokes.

'My mother tried to pacify me, saying that my mother-in-law had not said a word about Ronith. I did not know whether to cry or laugh.

'"Is that all?" I asked. "Just because I am thin, is it a good enough reason to break an engagement? As a person, am I of no importance to Aaron?"

'My mother was taken by surprise when I shook a fist at her and told her I would not allow Aaron or his family to play around with my life. I was sure they made fun of me behind my back and called me names like "scarecrow" and "the third part of the toddy tree". If they did not like me, why did they have the engagement ceremony?

'My mother was crying and telling me, "This is no laughing matter, you will be ruined," because a broken engagement is a stigma on a woman's life. I could not understand why my life would be ruined for no fault of mine, but for the fads of a fat boy who dreamt about a fat-bottomed wife.

'My mother tried to explain that nothing could be done in the matter and they had to start looking for another suitor for me. And that was going to be difficult, as once an engagement was broken, it was very hard to find a suitor for a young girl. It was easier for a man, not so for a woman.

'I stood facing my mother, holding on to the bag of gifts, saying, "Aai, you have two options: either you send me back to school and I will become a teacher and I promise to remain a spinster for the rest of my life, or you allow me to meet Aaron, just once, before the engagement is declared legally broken."

'My mother could not understand. "Why do you want to meet him?" she asked me. "After all, he is the one who has rejected you."

'I tried to convince her that I wanted him to tell me that he really did not like me. Suddenly my mother was furious. "How can you even think of speaking to him when he does not like you?"

'But I insisted on meeting him. I argued that if I was old enough to be engaged, I could also take my own decisions. I wanted to speak to Aaron, face to face.'

Rachel was roasting the puranpolis as she told Zephra the story of her engagement. Her daughter watched her with respect, feeling proud that, even as a girl, her mother had been strong enough to fight tradition. And, since the synagogue incident, she understood that her mother was a born fighter.

Offering a puranpoli to Zephra, Rachel continued, 'I did not allow my mother to return the gifts. Instead, I asked her to send a message to my in-laws: that, before the final decision was taken, I wanted to invite my fiancé for dinner. After all he was my cousin, not my enemy. I forced my mother to use exactly these words. Purim was just around the corner and it was decided that Aaron would have lunch with us.

'On Purim afternoon, he came to our house, dressed in a pale-blue, long-sleeved shirt and black trousers. He was polite and friendly, behaving as though nothing had happened. The only difference was that he kept his eyes averted from me and did not look straight into my eyes, as he normally did.

'I had requested my mother to leave us alone in the kitchen. I was sitting on the floor and making the puranpoli. He was sitting opposite me with lowered eyes, not saying anything, obviously embarrassed after what he had said and done.

'Rolling a puranpoli, I looked up and smiled. I noticed he was looking at me as though he was seeing me for the first time. I was wearing a bright-pink skirt, a brocade blouse and an embroidered silk sari. Sitting on the floor, I knew I was looking plump.

'Suddenly I felt his eyes were on me and he was asking, "Did you say something?"

'I just shook my head, and offered him a puranpoli dripping with ghee. I continued rolling the puranpoli, served him one and asked, "Did you like it?"

'He smiled, nodded and continued eating.

'I sighed loudly and said, "But you do not like me any more?"

'He looked up at me, his mouth full, and said, "I never said that."

'I asked, "Didn't you? You seem to have forgotten. A few days ago, your mother came here to break the engagement, just because you thought I was too thin."

'He was fumbling over his words and trying to explain. "Thin? I never said anything like that. I only told mother that I would have been happier if you were a little plumper. And, like all mothers, she thought I did not like you, so it was better to break the engagement. And I made the mistake of saying, do as you please. That is why she came here. Believe me, I did not realize that it would become so serious. When my mother returned home saying that she had broken the engagement, I was shocked and did not know what to do, as that had not been my intention. Don't I know, it will be difficult for you to find another suitor, considering that we have been engaged since we were children? Actually, I cannot see you married to anybody else but me. But I did not know how to handle the situation after mother had broken the engagement. I still do not know how to solve this problem."

'Sensing the seriousness of the situation, I stopped rolling the puranpoli and, wiping my hands, asked, "Do you really like the puranpoli?"

'"Yes," he smiled.

'"Take one more," I said.

'He ate one more, telling me about his dreams and his plans for our future together. By then, he had eaten about six puranpolis one after another. While he was on his sixth, he noticed that I had not eaten anything. So he asked me for one more puranpoli, and do you know what he did?

'He broke it into half and fed me with his own hands. Then, he bent towards me, and our lips touched just for a second—yes that was our first kiss,' Rachel blushed, 'and I knew I had nothing to worry about as he asked me to wear my engagement ring. By the way, it was then that I noticed that he was still wearing his!

'Casually, I called out to mother for the ring and wore it, smiling at her mischievously. And as a truce with my mother-in-law, I packed some puranpolis in a dabba for her. She would understand.

Aaron was smiling and my heart was beating so loudly that I was afraid he would hear my heartbeats. So I covered my breasts with the end of my sari to muffle the sound, looked up and knew we loved each other.

'Aaron said, "If your parents had not invited me for Purim, our lives would have been a mess."

'That year, before the wedding, I tried hard to put on weight, sometimes even wearing starched saris and heavy silks and brocades. One of my friends even taught me how to wear rouge, so that my cheeks looked fuller. But nothing worked. In fact your father thought I looked like a red-faced monkey and said he liked me the way I was. Thin or fat was no longer important.

'After our marriage, I discovered the way to your father's heart was through his stomach. And, so my dear Zephra, I have a soft corner for puranpoli. They bring love and happiness.'

Zephra understood the meaning of her mother's words.

BIRDA

Ingredients: val beans or field peas, oil, turmeric, onion, fresh coriander leaves, green chillies, garlic, cumin, coconut, salt

Method: Soak one cup val beans overnight. Choose the bitter variety for this recipe. Next morning, drain and hang in a muslin cloth bag. Val beans take two days to sprout, so make sure the bag is damp.

When the val beans sprout, remove from cloth bag and soak for half an hour in warm water, remove, dry and blanch.

Pressure cook the val beans for half an hour and keep aside.

Take a pan, heat one tablespoon oil and brown one chopped onion. Add a teaspoon garlic paste, two crushed green chillies, a pinch of turmeric, half teaspoon cumin, salt to taste and a few coriander leaves. Allow the masala to simmer on a slow fire, till it absorbs the oil. Add val beans and a glass of water and cook for ten more minutes. Add half a cup of coconut milk and cook on slow fire to thicken the

gravy. Garnish with fresh coriander leaves and serve
hot with sweet puris.

   Optional: Serve with lemon, as it adds to the taste.

❦

*Birda is pronounced 'bidda'. This recipe is prepared on the ninth
of Ab, for birda cha apvas. The meal is made to break the fast for
the fall of the first temple. Sprouting beans symbolize survival.
Jews have been persecuted through ages, yet they continue to
grow in numbers.*

Zephra woke up with a desire to eat something bitter, like
birda. Rachel used to make it for the fast of Tisha be Av.
Having eaten puranpolis the night before, Zephra wondered
whether her mother had added a secret ingredient in the filling
which attracted her to Judah. Perhaps Rachel knew magic potions
like the one she had used to ensnare her reluctant fiancé.

   Zephra blamed her mother for feeling the way she did. She
was embarrassed that her eyes often locked with Judah's. At this
particular point in life, she did not want a romance. She had
rushed to India just to lend support to her mother, not to fall in
love with her lawyer. While talking to him, Zephra heard her
heart beating wildly, exactly as Rachel had heard hers when Aaron
had kissed her. Annoyed with herself, Zephra cut short their
conversation and left the room. She was certain the puranpolis
were made with an aphrodisiac. What else would explain why
she felt the way she did?

   Judah was amused when Zephra left her sentence halfway and
disappeared into the house. He was in love with Zephra. When
he had eaten a morsel of Rachel's famous puranpoli, he knew
that he desired Zephra. If he got a chance, he wanted to tell her
how he felt about her before she left for Israel.

   That afternoon Zephra decided to keep away from Judah and

took a walk on the seashore. She remembered the hurt she had felt when Zvi left her. Kicking a shell in the sand, she remembered how her dreams had crashed around her. Perhaps that was the reason she was afraid of falling in love with Judah. She had become defensive about men since her brothers and sisters-in-law were always introducing her to every possible prospective Bene Israel suitor in Israel.

But Zephra knew instinctively that, try as she may, she could not keep away from Judah, at least not for long. She walked barefoot on the beach, dodging the crabs, and did not see Judah walking towards her. Suddenly she was face to face with him. And, as though it was the most natural thing on earth, she did not resist when he took his hand in hers and said, 'Zephra, I love you.' She did not stop him when he took her in his arms and kissed her, at first tenderly, then passionately.

Rachel saw them from her chair on the veranda, half asleep, half awake, wondering whether it was a dream. She had often imagined her daughter would fall in love with a young man like Judah. She closed her eyes and thanked the Prophet Elijah. He had heard her prayers.

With a wicked smile spreading on her wrinkled face, she knew the puranpoli had worked on Judah the way it had worked on Aaron. She went into the kitchen and saw that the val beans had germinated. 'A good omen,' she told herself. 'May the tribe increase.' So, while making the dough for the puris, she added a little more jaggery, making the puris sweeter than usual. Anyway what was life, if it was not a little bitter, a little sweet and a little sour?

That night, as she served the hot puris with the birda, Rachel noticed that Zephra looked disturbed, but Judah was eating with obvious pleasure. Zephra suddenly realized that she was not helping her mother and, taking the zhara from her hand, ordered Rachel to sit down and eat. She rolled the puris, fried them and served them to both Rachel and Judah.

Rachel was amused and silently she blessed the youngsters.

KANAVALI

Ingredients: semolina, butter, ghee or vegetable ghee, coconut, cardamom, sugar, salt, raisins, almonds

Method: Take a pan and brown half a kilogram of semolina in two tablespoons ghee or vegetable ghee or butter, and keep aside.

In another casserole, heat one tall glass coconut milk on a slow fire and add four tablespoons sugar with a pinch salt. Slowly, fold semolina in this mixture, stirring continuously till all liquid evaporates. Add six crushed cardamom seeds, a few blanched almonds broken into small pieces and fifteen raisins. Cover and cook for five more minutes. Transfer this mixture in a greased dish, place in an oven and bake on medium heat for ten minutes, till golden brown.

If you do not have an oven, pour mixture in a thali or platter, cool, cut into diamond-shaped pieces and serve.

Optional: Add four tablespoons jaggery instead of sugar.

If made on Friday afternoon, kanavali or Sabbath cake is a wholesome meal for the Sabbath. If it is to be served with meat dishes, Bene Israel Jews make kanavali in vegetable ghee, or else they prefer to use pure ghee.

Judah woke up early, made his tea, carried his cup to the veranda and looked out for Rachel. She was not there, but the birds had been fed, the ducks were swimming in the pond, the goat was grazing in the yard, a bowl of milk was kept under the chair for Brownie and the cat was sitting on the window sill, licking her paws. Everything was neat, organized and peaceful.

Judah settled down in a chair and assumed Rachel had gone down the road to buy vegetables. He needed to speak to her. He was not sure if she already knew that he was attracted to Zephra. Perhaps she had seen them kiss on the seashore.

Judah sipped his tea and glanced through the *Raigadh Times*, but his thoughts kept going back to Zephra, sleeping in the next room. He looked at the closed door and wondered if he should wake her up with a cup of coffee. He hesitated, not sure how she would react. What if she had changed her mind and was no longer interested in him? Sometimes she scared him with her moods. But, then, would a woman kiss a man without being interested in him? Perhaps it meant nothing to her. He had his moments of doubt. What if she woke up, whispered a sleepy good morning and behaved as though nothing had happened the night before?

He had told her, I love you, and she had whispered something that sounded like I love you too. He was not sure. The day she had arrived, she had not closed the door of her room, and on his way to the kitchen he had seen her sleeping. She looked like a small girl in her tee shirt and shorts, sprawled out on her stomach, legs spread out, arms folded under the pillow. He shivered, imagining her sleeping next to him.

He left his cup on the table and picked up the newspaper again to divert his mind. But it did not help. Impatiently he threw it away and opened his office bag and pulled out a sheaf of legal documents.

He did not hear Zephra moving in the kitchen, till the fragrance of coffee hit him and he felt a light kiss on his cheek. He snuggled backwards; Zephra's arms were around his neck and his head rested against the softness of her breasts. She smiled and surprised him by kissing him and asking, 'How do you like your eggs?'

'Double fried in pure ghee with a glass of hot masala milk.'

'This can't be true,' said Zephra. 'That is exactly how my father liked his eggs. You better start accepting the fact that under all that hard-core lawyer facade, there is a typical Bene Israel male hiding somewhere inside you.'

'Actually, I like them with a strong dash of salt, pepper, red chillies and if possible mustard.'

'No mustard. We just have ketchup and puris, and stop ordering me around, I am not your wife.'

'You could be,' he said, pulling her back into his arms.

They had their breakfast on the veranda. He ate his eggs and she nibbled at a dry toast. 'Losing weight,' she smiled.

'You are perfect,' he said.

'If I start getting fat at this rate, you won't like me any more.'

'Now, let me look at you. You are rather on the plump side, taller than most girls, but your temper is on the short side.'

'And I never saw anybody with such devilish green eyes.' Then, looking around the house, she asked, 'But where is Mama? If she sees us kissing and talking like this, she will make sure that we get married tomorrow.'

'Why not? Where is she?'

'No idea. Maybe at the synagogue, to see that everything is in order and the mice are not playing with the menorah. Even in her sleep, she sees things happening in the synagogue. She is afraid that one morning she will wake up and it won't be there.'

'I have to do something as soon as possible. Why don't you call your friend Kavita Chinoy?'

As she reached for the phone, Zephra saw an autorickshaw

stop at the gate, and Rachel walking towards the house with bags of food.

She ran down the steps to help her, saying, 'Mama, why do you have to buy so much food? We ate so well last night and there are still so many puris left over from last night's dinner.'

Rachel raised her chin obstinately. 'I don't have my daughter here every day. Bas, today I felt like cooking.'

'You say that every day, don't you?'

Sorting the packets of food on the kitchen platform, Rachel told Zephra that she had picked up some trotters from Hassaji Daniyal and she would make a shorba. She had everything that she wanted for the evening, but not the naan. It would be ready at Rustom bakery around four in the afternoon. Zephra offered to pick them up.

Washing the trotters in the kitchen sink, Rachel saw that Zephra and Judah were holding hands and deep in conversation. She wanted to see Zephra married while she was alive and did not like the idea of an unmarried daughter living alone and abandoned in a faraway land. She wondered, if Zephra married Judah, would she return to Israel or settle in Bombay? Because Judah was comfortable in India and never spoke about Israel, even as a joke. And Zephra had been living in Israel since she was eighteen and was now planning to study archaeology, after having spent a large part of her young life on a kibbutz.

Sifting the semolina in a bowl, Rachel worried and wondered whether they would settle in India or Israel. Then, crushing the cardamom seeds in a brass pestle, she left their fate in the hands of the Prophet Elijah.

When Judah was preparing to leave for Bombay, Rachel objected with a loud, 'Nako, are you going back to your office? Even if you leave now, you have to promise to return for dinner. Why do you think I am making a shorba?'

'That, you are making for your daughter.'

Rachel corrected, 'Today is the Sabbath.'

Zephra smiled. 'Mama, why are you trying to convert this demon into a human being?'

Pleased with their bantering, Rachel put away the food in the refrigerator and looked forward to a quiet day with her daughter.

Zephra undid her hair, saying, 'Mama, rub some oil in my hair. I am going to wash it today.' Mother and daughter sat on the steps of the house, Rachel dipped her fingers in a bowl of warm coconut oil and rubbed it into Zephra's hair, reminiscing about how it used to be, long and black.

Now, it was brown and streaked red.

After a simple lunch of dal and rice, they spent the afternoon gossiping about family and friends. Zephra did not say a word about Judah and Rachel left for the synagogue a trifle disappointed. She wanted her daughter to confide in her, but Zephra avoided talking about Judah. Rachel had seen them kiss the night before, but times had changed; perhaps a kiss did not necessarily lead to marriage.

Zephra took a short nap. She woke up feeling heady and happy. It was already late, and she could not possibly wash her hair, pick up the bread and also meet Judah at the harbour. So she quickly tied her hair into a ponytail, pulled on a pair of old jeans and ran out of the house to catch an autorickshaw to Alibaug.

Zephra bought the naan from the bakery, chatted with Rustomji, and at first did not notice Kavita, rolling down the tinted glass of her car and stepping out daintily, dressed in a lime-green salwar kameez and golden sandals. Zephra felt rotten in her old jeans, baggy tee shirt and oily hair plastered to her head.

They were walking towards the beach, talking about the synagogue, when Kavita noticed her distracted look and asked if she was waiting for Judah.

'Is it obvious?' asked Zephra.

'Yes,' said, Kavita.

Zephra smiled, but did not say anything.

When Judah arrived, he saw the two women from a distance

and decided that he still wanted to pursue the matter of the synagogue with Kavita Chinoy. Zephra also had something like that in her mind, so when Kavita offered to drop them home in her car she invited Kavita for the Sabbath dinner.

Rachel was more than happy to see Kavita.

As Kavita called her husband to inform him that she was eating with the Dandekars, Zephra disappeared into the bathroom to wash her hair. Rachel called out to her that it was too late in the evening to wash hair and she would definitely catch a cold. Zephra laughed and closed the door. Half an hour later she emerged, looking fresh and beautiful, dressed in a long, black dress with a slit at the calf, wondering if Rachel would be shocked. She was not. Through the years, she had got used to seeing Zephra in the most unpredictable dresses, except of course the sari. She had promised that before her departure she would wear a sari to please her mother.

When Rachel opened the lid of the shorba and its aroma spread around the house, Kavita understood that it was a special meal for a special occasion. Rachel covered her head with the end of her sari, lit the Sabbath candles and invited a rather reluctant Judah to say a blessing over the wine and the bread. He hesitated for a second and said the Kiddush with goblet of wine in hand, aware that at that moment he had become part of Rachel's family.

After dinner, Rachel sat cross-legged in her chair, chopping betel nut and offering it to everybody, expecting to continue with the dialogue about the synagogue. Zephra understood her mother's mood and sighed. Tonight she was in no mood for problems; she wanted to float in the timeless quality of the night, next to her mother, her lover, her friend and the sea. But she knew that soon she would have to leave. Disturbed, she decided not to think about it. She felt caught between two worlds.

Kavita was saying, 'When we met for the first time, I thought that I could not help you as I never interfere in my husband's business, but we could try. Remember, Judah told us about making a museum in the synagogue like the one in Amsterdam? I have something like this in mind. If you arrange for the initial funds, I can help you get some donations from friends.'

Judah agreed. 'We have to collect a good sum, as we have to offer a larger amount to the synagogue committee than what your husband has promised Mordecai.'

Passing the Sabbath cake around, Kavita said she would try to speak to her husband. 'Satish is a rational man,' she smiled mischievously, 'and, as Aunty often says, we women have to find ways and means of cajoling our husbands. If necessary, trick them with love, affection and bombil. You will not believe this, but Satish loves bombil. If I want anything from him, I just have to serve him a plate of bombil, and I can even get away with murder. Earlier I used to order them from a Konkani restaurant in Bombay, but since Aunty taught me the recipe, I make them myself.'

Rachel said, 'When you decide to speak to your husband, I will make the bombil and you pass them off as yours. What do you say? I will mix them with some special ingredients and he will be yours.' She smiled mysteriously.

They sat late into the night, talking about how they would use the money that Rachel had collected and the amount expected from Israel and Kavita's donor friends.

Once they had the synagogue, they were not sure what they would do with it. There was nobody there to look after it. Rachel was afraid: eventually it would become a ruin and some other person would take over the land, legally or illegally.

Judah was not willing to end the evening on a pessimistic note. 'The synagogue could be an ideal place to exhibit Jewish artefacts. I am sure the Jewish community would like to invest in an idea like this. We could write to the Jews of Bombay, Pune, Ahmedabad and Israel. Our synagogues in India have a lot of material stored away. We could ask them to donate anything and everything from old shofars to curtains to candle stands to old mezuzahs, Passover plates, kosher knives, circumcision knives and the hazzan's robe, which is no longer worn. We could collect everything to make our museum.'

Rachel shivered and, covering herself with a shawl, asked, 'You have brilliant ideas my son, but once I am dead and gone, who do you think is going to look after all this?'

Zephra moved closer to her mother and held her in her arms, not knowing what to say. Kavita watched Judah and Zephra, hoping they would get married and stay back in Danda. Judah looked away and Zephra did not say anything. They did not know where life would lead them, but somehow the fate of the synagogue depended on them.

So far no commitments had been made. Judah had not yet proposed to Zephra or even asked Rachel for her daughter's hand. Long ago, when Rachel had joked about it, he had not known that one day it would become a reality. Zephra lived in Israel and he lived in Bombay. How would they find a balance or a way of life between the two countries?

They sat listening to the sea, Rachel hoping the Prophet Elijah would find a solution for them. He had shown the way to the ancestors, who lay buried in the seven wells at Kehim beach. The sea was changing colour, the moonlight was cutting the waters, creating an illusion of a path on the surface of the water.

Judah stood up, saying, 'We will pass over that bridge when when we come to it.'

TILKUT POTATOES

Ingredients: potatoes, onions, tilkut, salt, oil

Method: Tilkut is made with two cups whole red chillies and one cup sesame seeds, ground in a mixer and bottled for six months.

In you do not want to make tilkut, cook potatoes with red chilli powder and sesame seeds.

Take six big potatoes, peel, cut into halves and then into thin slices. Cut two big onions into halves, slice and keep aside.

Take a big karhai or wok-style open-mouthed heavy- bottomed pan and heat seven to eight tablespoons oil. Fry potatoes on a high flame, stirring continuously till half done, lower flame, cover and cook for five to ten minutes. Add sliced onions, two teaspoons tilkut powder and salt, cover and cook till done. Drain excess oil and cook for five more minutes till crisp but soft.

Serve hot with khichdi or chapattis or a loaf of bread or plain dal—rice or as combination with dahikadhi and khichdi or with eggs, fried sunny side up.

Optional: Tilkut potatoes are delicious when cooked with a bouquet of chopped spring onions, added when potatoes are almost done. Garnish with sesame seeds.

Variation: Tilkut chutney is made with red chillies, salt to taste, sesame seeds, garlic, raw peanuts and served with chapattis, dal–rice or vegetables.

➸➔

We know it well, the food of exile and the seed of prosperity.

Rachel had bought the best bombils from the fishmonger and they were ready when Kavita came to pick up the tiffin carrier of food.

Rachel had put her heart and soul into the fish, hoping that it would speak to Satish Chinoy. She had also kept aside some bombil for Judah, hoping it would loosen his tongue and he would ask for her daughter's hand in marriage.

Already, she knew tongues were wagging in Alibaug. Whenever young, unmarried Bene Israel men and women were seen together, it was assumed they would get married or the boy's parents would initiate the manga or proposal for marriage.

Rachel knew she had to step in at some point and speak to Judah, as he did not have any direct family, but she hesitated, since she had already annoyed him, much before he had met Zephra. Now it was a different matter since they both liked each other. The night before, she knew, they had slept together.

It troubled her for a while, but then, drifting into sleep, she was relieved that he was there for Zephra. She was in the arms of a good, caring man. They made a handsome couple. In her dreams, Rachel saw them as bride and groom standing on the teva in the synagogue at Danda.

When the gossip reached Rachel, she did not care because she had herself scandalized the community by allowing them to stay together in her house. Yet she was in a bad mood. However open-minded she was, she wanted Judah to propose marriage to Zephra as soon as possible. Rachel felt gloomy and sensed that something untoward was to happen when she saw Rubybai's car stop at her door. She was relieved that Judah had left for Bombay and Zephra was in Murud-Janzira to meet an old school friend.

Rachel and Rubybai settled down as usual in the drawing room, as the chairs on the veranda were too small for Rubybai. With cups of tea and a plate of karanjias between them, they sat on the sofa.

If Rachel was small and thin, Rubybai was enormous: she had a large double chin like a bloodhound, small eyes and layers of fat rolling down from her chest to stomach. She wore loosely draped chiffon saris, long-sleeved blouses and diamonds. Rachel liked her as she was kind-hearted and had been Rachel's friend since they were children. But she disliked it when Rubybai wanted to know all that Rachel did not want to say.

Rachel saw that Rubybai was eager to talk about Zephra and her marriage and for nothing on earth was she going to miss the juicy details. She wanted to know everything before anybody else.

Rachel bristled as Rubybai reminded her, 'You have always confided in me. And now when Zephra has decided to get married, you don't want to tell me anything. Am I not your best friend?'

Rachel was crestfallen. 'I don't know about marriage, but I know they like each other.'

Rubybai was furious. 'Are you blind or something? Your daughter is the topic of conversation in the entire Raighad district and you say you don't know anything!'

Rachel sat hands folded in her lap, saying nothing, as Rubybai continued with her monologue. 'My children also live in Israel, but when they are here, do they smoke or wear shorts, wear dresses with slits or do they go hand in hand with a stranger on the Alibaug beach? I believe they kiss in public and you are trying to tell me there is nothing. From when did you become so modern?'

Rachel's pursed her lips and said, 'You are insulting me.'

'I am not. I am trying to help. Oh, come on Rachel, I have come to celebrate. Where are the sweets?'

'Listen, there are no sweets, because you just called Judah a stranger.'

'He is. Have we seen him before? If he is a Jew, he must have some interest in the community.'

'He has. Isn't he helping me with the synagogue?' Rachel asked, trying hard to keep her cool.

'That is true . . .'

'This is enough,' said Rachel sternly. 'I refuse to talk about him. Why should anybody bother about my daughter's habits like smoking or her clothes, as long as I am not bothered?'

'Sorry Rachel. I did not mean to criticize Zephra, but, for years, we have been following some traditions in Danda.'

'What tradition? Do you even know what your kids do in Israel? At least, Zephra does not hide anything from me—that is more important than anything else. And, if we send them there, they will cultivate new habits and new lifestyles, which we have to accept. If and when Zephra decides to get married, I will tell you.'

Defeated, Rubybai's chest heaved and she changed the subject to other matters.

To add insult to injury, that afternoon, after Rubybai left, Kirtibai called, asking if she needed help for the wedding preparations. Rachel knew that Kirtibai was a simple woman and not involved in the Alibaug politics, so she just laughed it off, but was nevertheless annoyed.

What a small world we live in, she thought. But she did not show her annoyance to Kirtibai, as she was always there for her. Yet, sometimes, when it came to family matters, it was hard to be nice to old friends.

Rachel sat staring at the synagogue, the root of all her problems. If she hadn't invited Judah to help her with its legal problems, he wouldn't be there and Zephra wouldn't have rushed down from Israel and the two would have never met.

When Zephra returned from Murud-Janzira, she saw her mother sitting in her deckchair on the veranda. It worried her, as she was neither cooking nor flitting between the house and the synagogue. She touched her mother's forehead, asking if she had a fever.

'Nothing,' she said. 'Just sit down here. I want to speak to you.'

From the harshness in her voice, Zephra understood it was about Judah and marriage. So, to give herself time, she went to her room and changed into a pair of shorts and a tee shirt. She resented the fact that her mother should speak to her as though she were six years old and had not done her homework. But, then, since she had grown up, Rachel had rarely got angry, so Zephra gave her the liberty of motherly concern. She had also seen in her mother's eyes that she knew she was in love with Judah.

She also saw that in her eyes it was a crime to be intimate with a man before marriage. She did not know how to explain to her mother that she was not a virgin and Judah was not the first man in her life. There had been others and she had lived for five years with Zvi.

That is what she had told Judah the night before. They had confided in each other. There were no secrets between them. Perhaps it was stupid of them to have slept in the same house as Rachel and it was but natural that Rachel expected them to get married as soon as possible. But, then, something more powerful, beyond their control was pulling them towards their destiny. In a way Zephra was glad that Rachel wanted to speak to her. It would be easier to voice her worries, fears and desires.

Zephra went into the kitchen and was surprised that there was nothing to eat. She was hungry and also wanted to kill some more time, so she made a quick tomato soup with some old puree she found in the fridge. Rachel refused the bowl of soup; instead she stood up and shouted at Zephra for the first time in years.

'Get out of those knickers and wear something decent.'

Zephra was expecting something like this to happen, but kept her calm. With unsteady hands she kept the bowl of soup on the table and asked, 'Mama do you really mind if I wear shorts?'

This only infuriated Rachel. 'Does it matter any more?' she snapped. 'Yes, it does matter in the Jewish community. For them, you are a juicy topic of conversation, wearing such clothes, showing your legs, walking hand in hand with Judah, kissing him on the beach and what not. What are you up to? This is India, not Israel.'

Zephra looked at her mother defiantly, her temper rising. 'I am here to be with you. I don't care a damn for the community.'

'Even if you don't, they are part of my life.'

'Mama, we tried to take you with us to Israel—you always refused. You do not even like to talk about it. You know, as children we feel guilty of abandoning you and leaving you here, alone in India.'

'I know, but I cannot leave.' Rachel was sobbing.

Zephra sat next to her, feeling helpless, and holding her hand. 'Mama, please,' she whispered, 'I didn't mean to hurt you. This is the way I am. Look at all those dances in Hindi films and these girls in Bombay and Delhi—they wear even less and I have seen couples holding hands and kissing everywhere. So what's new about me?'

'Then why don't you tell me what is going on in your life?' Rachel appeared to soften.

'I will, when the time comes.'

'What time? Zephra, don't cheat me, I know, last night . . . why don't you tell me . . .?'

'Must I tell you that I love Judah? But Mama, I am not sure. We like each other very much, that's it.'

'What about marriage?'

'That is a difficult question to answer. Yes, we love each other, but have not yet spoken about marriage. Actually, I am afraid to get married.'

Rachel wiped her face with the end of her sari. 'If you love each other, marriage is the next step, nako?'

'Nako,' said Zephra, 'loving and living are two different matters.'

'You talk like a philosopher!'

'It is the truth.'

'But you like Judah, don't you?'

'Not "like". I love him and could marry him, but it is too early to say when.'

'Then do me a favour, as long as you are here, let us keep it a secret. It is very hard for me to answer people.'

'People?'

'Kirtibai called and Rubybai drove down from Alibaug just to ask me about you and Judah.'

'Does it matter, Mama?'

'Yes.'

'Mama, please come to Israel. It must be tiring to live in India and be answerable for everything.'

Rachel was thinking. 'We will see, but you must get married.'

'I will.'

'When?'

'When I feel I am ready.'

'What's wrong with getting married to Judah now?'

'Because I am afraid.'

'Afraid of what? Judah is a good man.'

'What if it does not work?'

'Nothing works. You have to make it work day after day.'

'But I live in Israel and Judah appears to be rooted here.'

'So what? If you love each other, you can live anywhere as long as you are together.'

'How can I be comfortable in India, after all these years in Israel?'

'You can try.'

'Do you think Judah would leave India?'

'Ask him.'

'What if he does not?'

'When two people want to be together, everything works out.'

Zephra was watching the synagogue, the sun was behind it and the light had made a halo around it. In a strange way, the synagogue had brought her to Danda and it would surely show her the way. Then, pointing at the picture of the Prophet in the drawing room, she asked, 'Does the Prophet Elijah listen to our prayers?'

'Sometimes he listens, if he has the time,' Rachel smiled.

Then Zephra did something which her rational mind would have never allowed her to do: she called for a taxi, quickly dressed in a salwar kameez to please her mother and asked her to accompany her to the pilgrimage place or rock of the Prophet Elijah, Eliyahu Hannabi cha tapa.

It took a good hour from Danda to reach Sagav via Kandala.

The sun was about to set and there was a golden glow in the sky. The rock was shining in the half-light. The hoof mark cut across the rock like the mark of a silver sword. Rachel believed that the Prophet Elijah had flown to India in his chariot, on his way to heaven from Israel and, as he passed by, he had left his mark on the rock.

They stood under the flame of the forest, heads covered, eyes closed, hands clasped in prayer. Perhaps both had a different prayer or perhaps the same. They did not tell each other. Touched by the timeless quality of the Prophet's rock, they returned home in silence.

When they reached home, Rachel switched on the light and saw Judah sitting in the dark. He noticed they were in no mood to talk as Rachel gave him a weak smile and slumped in her chair, exhausted and hungry.

And for a change, Zephra started preparations for dinner. She decided to make khichdi and tilkut potatoes. In the fridge there was some soup she had made for lunch and pudding from the night before. She busied herself in the kitchen, while Judah sat next to Rachel, listening to the sea. Then Rachel heard a voice. She felt it came to her from somewhere far away, perhaps the horizon?

It was Judah, asking her for Zephra's hand in marriage.

Rachel smiled; the Prophet had heard her prayers.

MALIDA

Ingredients: dates, flaked rice or poha, sugar, coconut, almonds, pistachios, raisins, fruit, biscuits or cake, rose petals

❖

A malida is organized as an offering to the Prophet Elijah, Eliyahu Hannabi, for a secret wish fulfilment.

Normally the entire community is invited to partake in a malida ceremony or a minyan of ten men must be present for the ceremony.

The women of the house must be bathed, dressed in clean clothes and must wash their hands before starting preparations for the malida.

The malida platter consists of Ha'etz, Ha'adama and Bore mineh mezonaoth.

Ha'etz is fruit which has a hard trunk, like dates. Ha'adama is fruit with soft trunks, like banana, chikoo, grape, orange, sweet lime, melon and mango when in season. Bore mineh mezonaoth consists of wheat preparations like biscuits and cakes.

The dates and fruit must be cleaned, washed and wiped with a clean cloth. Fruit can vary from apple, chikoo, mango, pineapple, banana, orange and pomegranate to sweet lime. Bananas are washed, wiped and cut into three to four bite-size pieces. Pineapples, melons, apples and chikoo are peeled and sliced. Oranges and sweet lime are peeled, cleaned of seeds and veins. Grapes are washed and wiped clean. Mangoes are peeled and sliced. The skin of the pomegranate is removed and seeds served with the other fruit.

Flaked rice—poha—is cleaned, washed, soaked in water, drained, mixed with coconut and garnished with raisins and chopped nuts.

Red roses are also washed and kept aside for the baraka or blessing of sweet fragrance and a petal each is offered to those present. Sometimes an entire pomegranate is placed in the centre of the malida platter as a symbol of unity or its seeds are sprinkled over the poha.

The malida platter is placed on a clean white tablecloth and covered with a decorative textile, either cotton, silk, crotched or embroidered.

When the Eliyahu Hannabi prayers begin, a member of the family brings the platter to the teva and the cantor, hazzan or rabbi says a blessing over it. After this the platter is taken back to an anteroom, where women prepare a plate per person with dates, pieces of fruit, two tablespoons of prepared poha, a biscuit or piece of cake.

Rose petals are either placed in each plate or offered to the congregation.

The congregation moves to another room or to a courtyard, where the malida plates are served. Blessings are said over the Ha'etz, Ha'adama and Bore mineh mezonaoth. The malida normally starts with Ha'etz, the date, a symbol of the Promised Land, followed by Ha'adama and ends with Bore mineh mezonaoth. A malida is normally followed by a dinner and festivity. The reason of the wish or the malida is never revealed nor questioned.

Zephra knew that Kavita was in Alibaug. But, try as she may, Zephra could not find her: her mobile was switched off. Again, she tried calling her several times in Bombay and Alibaug, and was told memsaab was not there. Zephra even took an autorickshaw and went to their farmhouse and asked the chowkidar if Kavita was there. He said that nobody was at home. Zephra left messages on all Kavita's numbers and returned disappointed.

That was unlike Kavita. Zephra had the premonition that something was wrong. Perhaps Kavita had not been able to convince her husband and did not have the courage to tell them the truth.

Not willing to face Rachel, she took an autorickshaw to Kehim beach to take a walk around the wells of the ancestors. The tall silhouette of the monument to the dead rose towards the sky and could be seen from a distance, against the backdrop of the sea with the two fatal rocks, Chanderi–Underi, where the ships of the ancestors had wrecked.

There were seven wells under one mound, holding the secret of their ancestors. Seven couples who had survived the shipwreck, encased in the womb of the earth. She was a seed of this ancient myth.

Walking among the harsh scrub, she felt deeply moved. She had felt a similar emotion at the western wall in Jerusalem. This was her history and she was part of it. She sprinkled the mounds with roses, lit the candles and stuck them into the earth. 'Hear O Israel,' she was crying . . .

Zephra sat on the beach, watching the waves and wondering about the fate of the Bene Israel Jewish community of India. Almost the entire community had immigrated to Israel. The few who were left behind did not know where they were going and what they would do with their heritage of old, dilapidated synagogues. She felt her mother was fighting a losing battle.

On the way back to Danda, Zephra was thinking about her own life. She had accepted Judah's proposal of marriage, but they were not clear about their future. She was confused and for a second she even regretted coming to India.

On reaching home, she saw that Rachel was not in her chair, nor was she in the kitchen. Assuming that she was at the synagogue, she peeped into her bedroom and was surprised to see her sleeping in her bed, rolled up in her sari like a corpse. It was unlike Rachel. She touched her mother's forehead; it was cold. Rachel saw her and raised her hand, pointing towards the synagogue. Zephra looked out of the window and saw labourers constructing a wall around the synagogue and ran out to ask them what they were doing. The overseer said he had orders from Chinoysaab to build the wall.

Crestfallen, Zephra returned to the house to attend to her mother, who was complaining of chest pain. Not knowing what to do, she phoned Kirtibai and asked her to call their common family doctor. Kirtibai rushed to the house and took over from Zephra, called Dr Shinde in Revdanda, and sat next to Rachel, holding her hand and waiting for the doctor.

Zephra called Judah, and told him about the construction work around the synagogue. He left all that he was doing and rushed to Alibaug, to get a stay order from the Raigadh courts.

Waiting for the doctor, Zephra sat on the veranda steps, heart beating wildly and afraid of losing her mother. She was praying to the Prophet Elijah, asking him to help her. Since she had grown up so close to his rock edict, the memory of the Prophet often came back to her when she needed him. Her mother often reminded her, 'This is the land of the Prophet Elijah, nako?' She had never understood the meaning of these words as she did at that very moment. She even beseeched the ancestors to stand guard over her mother. Her own life was taking all sorts of turns and twists and she needed her mother, more than ever, nako?

Dr Shinde arrived, checked Rachel and said she had high blood pressure and that her cardiogram was rather unstable. He feared the onset of a heart attack. He gave her an injection and was in two minds about shifting her to the Alibaug civil hospital. After all, she was old and he could not take the risk of treating her at home.

Tense about her mother's condition, Zephra called her brothers in Israel. They were worried and were willing to leave for India, if she needed them. She told them to wait for one more night.

The synagogue stood in the distance and Zephra was angry with its silence. It had spelt doom in her little world. She did not need it any more.

After consulting the cardiologist at the civil hospital, Dr Shinde decided to shift Rachel, and Zephra sat biting her nails as they waited for the ambulance. Kirtibai made a glass of limbu paani for Zephra and forced her to eat a biscuit. How else was she going to look after her mother?

When the ambulance arrived, Zephra quickly packed a few clothes and left the house keys with Kirtibai so that she could feed Brownie and the birds. She sat in the ambulance holding Rachel's hand and noticed that she was distracted and trying to have a last look at the synagogue as they passed it. Zephra helped her raise her head, but knew, God willing, Rachel would return home to Danda.

Leaving her mother with the doctors in the intensive care unit, Zephra again called Kavita on her mobile, but received the no-reply signal. She returned to the ICU, hoping Judah would have a solution.

Word spread fast in Alibaug that Rachel was hospitalized. Rubybai, Hassaji Daniyal and others rushed there to help Zephra, who spent the whole day in agitation, not knowing what to do. The doctors assured her that Rachel would be better by evening.

The moment Rachel opened her eyes, she wanted to know about the wall around the synagogue. Zephra just shook her head and told her to rest.

Judah reached the hospital late that night. He looked harassed, not having made a headway at the Raigadh courts, but deeply concerned about Rachel. She opened her eyes, saw him standing in the doorway and raised her eyebrows in query. He gave her a reassuring smile and she closed her eyes and slept.

Judah and Zephra decided to spend the night in the waiting room. Without Rachel around them, they had nothing to say, nothing to do. Without her energy, they felt weak and helpless. She had been the driving force of their lives. Seeing her covered with a shawl and trapped in a maze of tubes, Zephra held onto Judah's hand. She needed to be comforted. She was dazed by the sequence of events, which had followed one another rather too quickly.

She did not want to spend a single minute away from her mother. Rubybai had returned to the hospital with food for Zephra and to see if Rachel was better and if they needed anything. With genuine warmth, she invited Judah to her house, for a meal and a good night's rest. Zephra's heart warmed to her.

When they left, Zephra stretched out on the sofa in the waiting room, but could not sleep. So she picked up a magazine and started reading. Slowly she dozed, then woke up with a start when she felt someone calling out to her. She sat up frightened, expecting the worst. A nurse was standing over her, asking if she was the daughter of the old lady who had been admitted in the ICU, as there was someone at the gate asking for her. Zephra guessed it was Kavita.

Kavita's car was parked in the foyer of the hospital. The driver opened the door and Zephra slid in the seat next to her. She no longer cared what had transpired between the Chinoys. All that mattered at that very moment was her mother's life.

Kavita held her hands and did not say anything. She did not want to give her false hopes. Anyway it was too late in the night. Yes, she had received Zephra's messages and could not answer as she had been closeted in her husband's office for hours. Satish had told her that Mordecai had approached him with an offer to sell the synagogue with the land around it. He had said it was his property and had papers to prove it. Satish thought it was the perfect locale for a seaside resort and did not want to lose the land around the Itzraeli synagogue at Danda. When he had made the deal, he had not known anything about Kavita's involvement in the matter.

When Kavita had told him that Rachel Dandekar was her friend Zephra's mother, he had been perturbed, but did not know what to do, as he had already made the part-payment. Mordecai was in a hurry to seal the deal and leave for Israel. But Satish Chinoy had had his doubts and sent the legal documents to his lawyer, before preparing the cheque for the final payment, which was a fairly large amount of money. Like all businessmen, he wanted to play it safe.

But it was hard for him to understand why Kavita was interested in this particular deal. He did not like to mix sentiment with business. It took her hours to explain all that had been happening there in context to the Dandekars. She wanted her husband to reconsider the deal, although the papers appeared to be legally correct. Perhaps Mordecai had used vile ways to transfer the land in his name, by showing fake proof that the land belonged to his great-grandfather who had donated a part of the land for the synagogue. It took her a whole day, but Kavita at last convinced her husband to stop the construction around the synagogue and reconsider the purchase of the land. Although, Satish Chinoy pointed out to her, if he did not purchase the land, somebody else would grab it. After all it was prime property.

Zephra listened like one numbed. Then rather hesitantly she told Kavita that Judah was about to bring a legal stay order on the construction work around the synagogue. He had also discovered from old records that a religious place like a synagogue or a cemetery could not be sold. According to law, it could only be converted into a public park or a garden. He had also discovered an old document, which could not be deciphered, but was probably a khat, or document, which said that the land had been given to the Dandekar family during Shivaji's rule as his fort was nearby on the seashore of Murud-Janzira.

Kavita asked Zephra to persuade Judah to not create a legal tangle, as she felt it would only complicate matters. She felt it was very important to organize a quick meeting between Judah and Satish. Zephra assured her that she would speak to him. She did not know that Judah had been waiting for some such opportunity to speak to Satish Chinoy.

When Kavita left, Zephra went zombie-like into the hospital, wondering how she would break this news to Rachel in the simplest possible way. She peeped into her room and saw that she was awake; she rested her head on her mother's hand, kissed her and whispered, 'The bombil worked. Come Mama, get well soon.'

Rachel smiled and again closed her eyes and slept.

The next morning, Rachel was better. Judah and Rubybai arrived early with a flask of coffee for Zephra. She left her mother in Rubybai's care and returned with Judah to Danda.

In the autorickshaw Zephra told him all that had transpired between Kavita and her husband and, as proof, they saw that Kavita had convinced her husband to stop the construction around the synagogue. Yet, Judah was agitated, and wanted to plan his next move carefully. The future was no longer important—the present was. Every single minute was precious. He had to make his next move before Mordecai made his.

Zephra called her brothers, who were waiting for news. They were relieved to hear that Rachel was better. Both brothers had dispatched large donations to the bank in Alibaug. If need be, they were ready to leave for India if Rachel got worse or Judah needed their help.

Kirtibai arrived with a tiffin carrier of food and to inquire about Rachel's health and help Zephra with Brownie, the goat, the ducks and the poultry. When she left, Zephra packed some clothes and toiletries, while Judah searched for the key to the synagogue, to see if he could find some more documents from the storeroom. They looked all over the house for the key. Zephra wondered if they were still tied to Rachel's pallav. Exhausted,

Judah sat on the verandah, looking through the papers Rachel had initially given him. Zephra went back to look for the keys in her mother's room, and she saw something shining on the window sill next to her mother's bed. They were Rachel's keys. Zephra felt a certain sadness creep over her as she looked at the bunch of keys in all shapes and sizes attached to a hook, sitting all alone on the window sill. Rachel and the keys were inseparable: only when she went for a bath did she leave them on a rack. In the morning light, the metal hook had a sinister glow. It was unlike Rachel to forget her keys. Since childhood, Zephra had always associated the jingle of keys with Rachel. Left alone on the window sill, they appeared lifeless. Zephra picked up the keys and held them in her palm. They meant so much to her. They were like a part of her mother's body.

For a second she panicked: perhaps they were her mother's talisman for good health. She wanted to rush back to the hospital and tie them to her sari. She was sure they were the keys to her revival.

Zephra studied the keys. They looked mismatched in a variety of metals. Some were rusted, others useless. The synagogue key was the largest. Big, long, flute-like, it seemed to proclaim its identity with its mere length.

Voice hoarse with emotion, Zephra called out to Judah. He stood in the doorway, watching her holding up the keys. He understood, and comforted her, holding her tenderly in his arms. Then, quickly, he walked towards the synagogue and turned the key in the lock. As usual, at first it resisted, then turned. When he opened the doors, he stood still for a moment, overcome with the beauty of the ancient monument. Full of light, it was shimmering in the morning light. By now, he knew the synagogue well, since he had often been there with Rachel. Not wanting to waste time, he made neat bundles of the rest of the papers and brought them back to the house. He was amused that, even after Mordecai had registered the land on his name, he had never thought of taking away the documents or the keys. He also knew that Judah was a lawyer, but had assumed that he was more interested in Zephra than in the synagogue.

Returning to the house, he gave the keys to Zephra and asked her to take them to Rachel. He stayed back, going through the documents and waiting for a phone call from Kavita.

When Zephra reached the hospital, Kavita was sitting next to Rachel. She had brought flowers, which the nurse had arranged in a vase. There were two flasks, one with coffee for Zephra, another with sweet-lime juice for Rachel, and a basket of food. With a sigh of relief, the first thing Zephra did was tie the keys to Rachel's sari. Her keys would defeat death.

Rachel touched them with her long, bony hands and played with the synagogue key, caressing it tenderly as she dozed. Kavita signalled to Zephra that she needed to talk to her. Kavita had arranged a lunch meeting for Satish and Judah that very afternoon, so they called Judah from Kavita's mobile.

That afternoon, the doctors checked Rachel's blood pressure and gave her permission to return home. With sheer relief, Zephra slumped in a chair and cried. She thanked the Prophet Elijah for bringing her mother back to Danda.

But, before taking her mother back home, she had an errand. It was to meet Hassaji Daniyal and request him to say the prayers to Eliyahu Hannabi, thanking the Prophet for saving her mother's life.

She also asked Rubybai to help her prepare the malida and arrange for a minyan of ten Jewish men.

As the ambulance sped towards Danda, Zephra knew that the malida would be held at the synagogue and she would serve a traditional dinner of chicken curry, chauli beans, saffron rice, sandan and coconut laddoos.

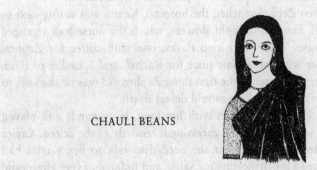

CHAULI BEANS

Ingredients: chauli beans (black-eyed beans), oil, onion, ginger, garlic, tomato, turmeric, chilli powder, cumin, coconut, coriander, salt

Method: Wash and soak a cupful of chauli beans overnight. Next morning, drain, wash and pressure cook or cook in a pan till done.

Heat two tablespoons oil in a casserole and brown one big onion, chopped into small pieces, add a teaspoon ginger–garlic paste and cook on slow fire. Add one big tomato, chopped fine, a pinch turmeric, half a teaspoon each of red chilli powder and cumin, and stir well. Add beans and cook for ten minutes in the masala. Add a tablespoon grated coconut, mix well and cook for five more minutes; add salt to taste. Garnish with fresh coriander leaves and serve hot with rice.

❈

Chauli beans are like a staple diet for Asian and Bene Israel Jews. Beans are served on festive occasions like circumcision, engagement ceremonies or for dinner which follows a malida.

Rachel looked out of the window from her bed. The activity around the synagogue reminded her of the days before the Aliyah or the great immigration of Jews in the sixties.

Zephra had brought down the chandeliers with the help of Hassaji and sparkled them with the glass spray Aviv had sent for his mother. Rachel breathed deep into her cologne-soaked handkerchief, wondering if the spray was similar in fragrance to Aaron's lavender aftershave lotion.

The electrician was replacing bulbs and making the fans work. Zephra had asked him to check all lights, repair all loose ends and ensure the safety of the electric fittings, which had not been in use for a long time. She dreaded a sudden accident or short circuit. A carpenter was polishing the tables, chairs and benches. The marble on the wall was being waxed, and like a circus artist Judah had made himself a scaffold to clean the marble plaque of the Ten Commandments written in English and Marathi. Hassaji Daniyal wiped clean the marble mezuzah, polished it with wax and decorated it with a rose.

Almost every possible drape had been removed. Some had been sent for dry cleaning; others were being washed, ironed or brushed. The curtain covering the Ark was removed and a tailor was mending it and some women were redoing the damaged embroidery around the Hebrew letters.

Rachel regretted that she had not got down to buying yardage for a new curtain; she had wanted to embroider it herself. She promised herself that she would make a new curtain for the approaching New Year prayers, blue like the summer sea and embroidered with silk and gold threads.

Zephra's band of workers were washing the tiles and removing the ancient cobwebs, woven like black clouds in the high-domed ceiling. Menorahs, candle stands and other brass artefacts were being scrubbed with warm tamarind water, exactly the way Rachel cleaned her brass. Silver goblets were given a good shine and the anterooms were aired, the cupboards cleaned and all the old textiles washed, brushed and repaired. In the process, Zephra salvaged some beautiful platter-covers in satin and velvet. She also found a frayed silk robe, which Hassaji Daniyal said he used to wear while conducting prayers and weddings.

Kavita had sent her gardener with a variety of potted plants and seasonal flowers, to help Zephra beautify the courtyard.

A makeshift tent had been put up in the garden so that Hassaji Daniyal and his family could cook the malida meal. Utensils and dishes of all shapes and sizes were brought out from the synagogue storeroom and given a good scrub, wiped clean and kept on rented tables covered with white sheets. Zephra had asked Hassaji Daniyal to prepare a menu her mother relished. He decided to make green chicken curry, coconut rice, curried liver, chauli beans, gharries and laddoos. As an afterthought he added sandans to the menu, as he remembered that Rachel had often told his wife that, somehow, she could never get them right. This was the right occasion to serve her sandans, soft, spongy and savoury.

In the house, a little away from the scene of activity, Rubybai and the women of her house were preparing the malida under Rachel's supervision. When everything was ready, Zephra returned to the house and, throwing open the cupboard, asked Rachel if she wanted to wear any particular sari. Rachel sat up in bed and chose the aubergine-coloured nine-yard sari she had never worn.

'Blouse?' queried Zephra, looking through the neat pile, and was about to pull out a blouse of the same colour when Rachel surprised her by asking her for a green one.

'Green!' said Zephra. 'Mama, you are going to shock everybody. At your age women must wear sober pastel colours, nako,' she said, holding the two fabrics together.

Zephra marvelled at the speed with which she wrapped those endless yards around her thin frame, pulling one end between her legs and tucking it at the waist, then pleating another length and throwing it over her left shoulder. Rachel also asked for her box of jewels and wore a gold chain, six gold bangles, a watch and pearl earrings and slipped on a pair of new Kolhapuri chappals. She looked in the mirror and was satisfied with her reflection as she powdered her face with her favourite Yardley's lavender talc and touched her temples with cologne water of the same brand.

Leaving Rachel with Rubybai at the synagogue, Zephra left to dress.

Judah was already at the synagogue, wearing a white kippa he had inherited from his father, a clean white shirt and formal trousers. He looked like a decent Jewish gentleman. When Zephra returned, she saw that he was extremely uncomfortable and standing as though he was facing a firing squad.

There were more people present for the Eliyahu Hannabi than expected. Jewish families from Revdanda and Alibaug had driven down to Danda. Zephra had also invited Kirtibai, her family, the fishmonger and the artisans who had helped her clean up the synagogue.

It was Saturday night and there was a half moon in the sky, the sea was quiet and there was a minyan of ten men including Judah. There was Hassaji Daniyal dressed in the old purple robe and a blue kippa, his son, his grandson, Rubybai's two sons, three sons-in-law, and an American tourist, named Silberstein. Zephra saw them from the window, relaxed and dressed quickly.

When Zephra entered the synagogue, all eyes were upon her. She was dressed in a red sari with a gold border and a black blouse. She looked tall, stately and beautiful. Rachel did not tell her that it was her engagement sari. Judah threw a glance at her and then fixed his gaze on the chandeliers. He knew it was taboo to stare at women in the house of the Lord.

Mother and daughter smiled at each other. There was love and appreciation in their glance. Rachel had covered her head and, not knowing how to express her appreciation for her daughter, pinned a handkerchief on Zephra's head, whispering, 'The head must be covered when one enters a house of prayer.'

Rachel felt satisfied as she saw the synagogue was almost full and echoing with the chant of the Eliyahu Hannabi. When the prayers ended, they moved to the open courtyard decorated with strings of mango leaves and marigold flowers. There was a festive air as the food was being served to the tune of Israeli folksongs.

Suddenly there was a stunned silence, as all eyes turned to the gate. A car had stopped and they saw Kavita standing there with her formidable husband, Mr Satish Chinoy.

Zephra saw her mother's hand tremble. She held it in hers and whispered, 'They are our friends, nothing to worry.'

She then signalled to Judah to look after the other guests and went forward to welcome the newcomers. Finding two chairs, she filled their plates and sat next to them. She did not want any awkward moments, and felt better when Judah and the other men sat around Satish Chinoy, talking about the civic problems of Raigadh district. Not once did Judah or Chinoy mention their lunch meeting. The day Rachel had been discharged from the hospital, Kavita had arranged a lunch meeting between the two men as promised. The conversation over onion soup and garlic bread had been difficult, but as they moved to the fish, the tension had eased, and by the time they reached the cheese soufflé they had become good friends.

Before his meeting with Judah, Satish Chinoy had paid the signing amount to Mordecai and had decided to go ahead with the construction. He was in a hurry, as he wanted to start the resort before the tourist season. But after Kavita's request, he had instructed his engineer to stop work at the synagogue site, even though his lawyer had seen all the papers of land transfers and said there was nothing amiss. Judah read the papers and brought to his notice that, through the years, Mordecai had cleverly transferred the land to his own name. So, in principle, the land around the synagogue belonged to him and he had the right to sell it.

Judah was shocked that the trustees and the executive committee had turned a blind eye to Mordecai's evil exploitation of the synagogue. He assumed they were tired old men who did not have the time and energy for such matters. Anyway, what could they do with a dilapidated synagogue, which was of no use to the Jewish community?

Satish Chinoy had met the committee only once, because Mordecai dealt with him and he had thought that everything was above board. But, since he understood from Judah that all was not well, he assured him that he would think twice before going ahead with the deal.

Judah did not know where this was leading, but knew that once dialogue with Satish Chinoy was possible they would reach some agreement. Chinoy listened attentively, wondering what to do and not sure that he liked his wife's involvement in the matter.

Judah was relieved, as he understood that Chinoy was a cool-headed, calculating businessman who would find solutions in the most entangled matters. At the end of the lunch they parted, both feeling light and relieved.

Judah still had a task ahead: that of convincing Rachel. She was an intelligent woman who would catch him if he faltered even once. He had to be very clear about what he was going to tell her. She had come to trust Kavita, but she was still suspicious about Satish Chinoy's intentions. At the malida, when Chinoy thanked her for the dinner, she just offered him a limp hand, giving him a half-hearted smile.

Satish Chinoy had put the matter on hold, informing Mordecai that he could not buy the land immediately. He was cordial with the old alligator so that he would not suspect that he was having second thoughts or else he would immediately find another buyer and they would never know about his next move. Going through the sheaf of legal papers made by Mordecai's lawyer, the copies of which Satish had given him, Judah was aware that perhaps they were fighting a losing battle.

The day after the malida, Judah spent a whole day in his

Bombay flat, studying legal books and records to find a solution. If he failed, Rachel would lose faith in him.

Zephra checked on Rachel's bank balance, but knew that they needed much more money than what they had. She also needed a computer and the Internet if she wanted quick replies to her letters. So she spent the days with Kavita at her farmhouse, typing letters, posting them and sending e-mails to Jews all over India, Israel, Europe and America, hoping to collect funds and artefacts. Perhaps they could convert the synagogue into a Jewish museum. She was receiving favourable replies from Jews known and unknown from all over the world.

To start with, Zephra had to convince the president of the synagogue committee to call a meeting at their house in Danda and sell the idea of a museum. With Mordecai around, it was not going to be easy and she made inquiries about his possible date of departure. He was migrating, making an Aliyah on the law of return to the Promised Land, with funds raised after selling the land of the Lord.

And to confront the committee, Zephra needed tact, intelligence, affection, and a good bottle of whisky, served with home-made snacks prepared by her mother, if the Lord permitted . . .

MINCE CUTLETS

Ingredients: mincemeat (mutton or chicken), potatoes, onion, eggs, salt, chilli, turmeric, ginger, garlic, coriander leaves, breadcrumbs, oil

Method: To make the mince filling, pressure cook half a kilogram mincemeat for about ten cutlets. Heat oil in pan, brown one onion, chopped very fine, add one teaspoon ginger–garlic paste, a pinch turmeric, salt, half teaspoon red chilli powder or one crushed green chilli and one heaped teaspoon finely chopped fresh coriander leaves. Add pre-cooked mince and cook till dry. Keep aside and cool.

Boil eight potatoes, mash, mix with salt and keep aside.

Make lemon-sized balls and shape into cup-size puris in the centre of your plam, place tablespoon of mince filling in the centre, pinch ends, close, shaping like patties. Beat two eggs in another bowl, dip cutlet in egg, cover with breadcrumbs and shallow fry till golden brown in colour.

On festive occasions, Jews all over the world make mincemeat cutlets in one way or another.

The synagogue committee accepted Rachel's invitation for an informal meeting over drinks. Judah had informed them by phone that Rachel would send a vehicle to pick them up; they did not know that Kavita had arranged for a car to pick them up and bring them to Danda from the Navi Mumbai expressway.

Since Aaron had died, Rachel did not as a rule entertain guests for drinks or dinner and, if somebody came to see her, she did not invite them to her living room, but preferred to meet them in the open veranda, overlooking the sea.

Judah and Zephra had convinced her to invite the synagogue committee for drinks. According to tradition, she should have invited them to dinner, but then making conversation about the synagogue would have been impossible. Anyway, she had an excuse: that she had not invited them to dinner as she was unwell.

As Zephra was making preparations for the evening, Rachel asked her to make seating arrangements in the drawing room. It would be easier to talk about a difficult subject like the synagogue there.

Rachel took great care in the choice of her sari. It was the one she had forced Aaron to buy for Yom Kippur, the white sari with a gold border, worn with sandals Zephra had brought for her from Israel. She decided to look like a landowner and not the caretaker of the synagogue. She had also slipped on her gold bangles, a chain with the Star of David and a wristwatch. Her hair was pulled back into a neat chignon with jasmine flowers. She looked every bit the lady of the house. Rachel had also advised Zephra to wear a formal white pant suit with high heel shoes, and Judah was to serve the drinks, as he was now part of the family. She had warned both Zephra and Judah that she was going to introduce him as her daughter's fiancé. The matter was sealed.

Mordecai too came and Rachel shook hands with him in the same way that she welcomed the rest. Her expression did not change, but face to face with Mordecai she looked straight in his eyes as if she was reading his mind. He was so unnerved by her direct gaze that he averted his eyes. She chose a big leather chair for herself, which had come down to her from the ancestors and had been repaired several times; it resembled a throne. She sat in the centre of the room, looking like the queen of Danda.

Judah showed them in, asking polite questions about their trip from Bombay to Danda. When they settled down on the chairs, they were surprised to see Kavita Chinoy in the Dandekar household. She had arrived early to help Zephra prepare the plates, arrange the glasses, reheat and serve the snacks, fill the ice bucket and make sure that there was enough ice in the freezer.

Mordecai fidgeted in his chair. He noticed that Kavita Chinoy, dressed in a cool, blue sari, appeared to be at home in Rachel's house. He did not like it at all. He drummed his fingers on the armrest, wondering what was to follow. He did not trust the young lawyer and was annoyed when Rachel introduced him as her future son-in-law. While the others congratulated them with the traditional mazal-tov, he did not react.

The sun was setting over the Arabian Sea and long shadows were cast over the surface of the water. It was about seven, the lights were switched on and Judah served the scotch in style. He also poured a little brandy for Rachel, who raised her glass and much to their surprise wished them le haim. Judah poured a drink for himself, left it on the table, offered cigarettes to the older men, helped them light the cigarettes and then sat cross-legged on his chair, puffing away at his cigarette.

Kavita and Zephra passed around the plates of fish, chops, mince cutlets and brain fry, then sat down with the rest. As Rachel did not want Zephra to drink or smoke that evening, she sat quietly like a good Bene Israel girl, sipping a tall glass of orange juice with Kavita. They could not help but notice the manner in which Mordecai ate, relishing everything and praising Rachel's culinary skills. He was so nervous that he kept repeating how close he had been to Aaron, who never allowed him to leave without having lunch or dinner.

Jhirad, the president, had never taken an interest in the matters of the synagogue. He sat quietly for a while, then as the whisky and food started working on his head, he asked Rachel, 'I believe you have invited us here for a special reason, so, tell us, how can we help you?'

Rachel smiled. 'You are right. I have a list of questions for you. The first question is that I haven't paid my membership for years, so where and how do I pay? I wonder what happened to the synagogue committee, because they are supposed to collect the membership fees.'

Then, looking at each person, she asked pointedly, 'I do not even know who the treasurer is.'

She opened her handbag and pulled out a five-hundred-rupee note and offered it in their direction.

There was silence. Each was looking at another and wondering what to say. Judah had been quiet so far, only concentrating on filling their glasses. He was tense.

Jhirad pursed his lips and looked questioningly at Mordecai, urging him to answer. Mordecai asked Judah to pour him a large peg and said, 'Look Rachel sister, I have known you for many years. Ten, twenty, thirty, forty, countless isn't? Your husband was my best friend, right?'

Rachel sipped her brandy and said, 'About my husband, let us leave him out of the conversation. He was a good man, but never knew the difference between friend and foe.'

Nobody moved, nobody spoke, as Jhirad shuffled in his seat, looking for a match to light his cigarette. Judah immediately stood up and offered him one.

Mordecai continued, 'All right sister, I do not know why you are so angry with me. But I am well meaning and whatever I do is for the good of the community. Do you think I could do anything to harm you or your family? See, I know, soon there is a going to be a wedding in your family, and believe me I will be the first one to help you and do the entire running around. Just call me and I will be there.'

'Mordecai brother,' said Rachel, 'let us face facts. I have heard that you and I can no longer run around like teenagers. Do you really think you will come here and make arrangements for the wedding?'

'Here? I do not understand—here? How can you have a wedding here in Danda? You would have to get your daughter married in one of the synagogues in Bombay or Thane. In Danda where will you have a wedding ceremony? Unless you are planning a civil marriage. Even then you will have to go to Alibaug to the courts of Raighad district.' His tone was vicious.

Rachel looked straight at him, took the plate of samosas and offered him one. 'These are your favourites—please have one more.'

'That is like my sister,' he said, taking one and dipping it in a bowl of tomato chutney.

'Gas,' whispered Rachel to herself, 'hope he comes down with gas even before he reaches the harbour and hope his wife scolds him for breaking bread with farmers.'

Then smiling politely, she said, 'Don't I know how you love my food, especially the recipes I make with chana atta, like peethal.'

'Yes,' he said, shaking his head, 'that is one of my favourites. But, as I told you, my wife hates it. She calls it poor man's food. Yet, you must give us the recipe before we leave for Israel.'

'Of course. When are you leaving for Israel?'

'It will take time, but we will leave as soon as I finalize some deals.'

'Like?' she asked sternly.

'Some personal matters,' he said, moving uncomfortably in his chair as Rachel spoke in a loud voice. 'Going back to the topic of the wedding, my daughter will get married right here, in Danda.'

'Are you going to build a kuppa on the seashore?' Mordecai asked sarcastically.

'I can, but why should I, when I have the synagogue at my doorstep?'

'Synagogue?' asked the committee members in unison.

'Yes, my synagogue, our synagogue, the one you can see from that window.'

'But nobody can get married in a ruin. There is nothing, no hazzan, no minyan, nothing.'

'But it still has a committee. And my daughter can get married there.'

For the first time in years Mordecai did not know what to say and stared at her in disbelief. He did not like intelligent women, and this one had always annoyed him with her questions. Aaron should have married his fat cousin Ronith. In one of their drinking bouts, he had said he liked them fat. He did not deserve this bombil who was making life miserable for everybody. He sat with a fish bone in his hand, aching to hurt her.

Quickly Zephra offered him an empty plate and he left it there, thanking her profusely.

Jhirad, who was on his fifth peg by then, suddenly spoke. 'Sister Rachel, we have no synagogue, no committee. I am just the president in name, your husband Aaron was the vice-president, Joseph here is the treasure, Lael is in charge of cultural activities and Mordecai is the secretary. The hazzan, as you know, has become a community butcher of sorts and gives horse rides to children on the beach. And, as far as a shamash is concerned, we have never had one in years. The last one, I believe, died in Israel, a couple of years back. We are just volunteers of the Lord. There is a Trust, but the members died years back. And if you remember, Mordecai's great-great-grandfather, God alone knows how many years ago, received this land from the British or the Dutch. He has the papers. So in principle the land belongs to him. He has recently sold it to the Chinoy family. Good people. Look, Mrs

Chinoy is right here with you, she must have told you, they plan to develop the land as a health resort and make the synagogue a greenhouse to grow flowers. Anyway it is of no use to any of us. Actually it has become a burden,' he said, tapping his fingers on his armrest.

It was then that Kavita spoke, her face flaming red. 'Excuse me uncle, but I am here because I am a family friend.'

Mordecai moved uncomfortably in his chair, and face flushed with anger, he glared at Rachel. Then, turning to Kavita, his expression softened as he said, 'Sorry madam, Jhirad is talking about your husband. And, if I remember correctly, I had introduced you to Rachel sister, I did not know that you were family friends.'

Rachel looked at Kavita affectionately and corrected him. 'She is our guest, a childhood friend of my daughter's, but that is of no importance. I wish to speak about the committee. Obviously there is none, nor do you have trustees and, as brother Mordecai says, there is no synagogue. As far as the story goes about the British and the Dutch, I am sorry to inform you that the land was never given as a gift to Mordecai brother's ancestors. It was given to my family. Ours was a very illustrious family, the Dandekars. This land was given to Haeem Robenji Dandekar by Shivaji Maharaj,' she said, picking up a box from the side table and opening it and pointing towards the photocopy of a tattered piece of paper. 'This document will tell you that the land was given to our family. Unfortunately, my good husband told this story to Mordecai brother, who made it up as his own, assuming that we are a bunch of fools who do not know how to look after the land of the Lord.'

Then, turning to Jhirad, she said, 'If Mordecai brother is leaving for Israel, we must accept his resignation. Also, please try to get the death certificates of the trustees who left us long back, and let us make a new beginning with the Trust deed. At least you have that?'

Jhirad sat wondering, 'Now where is the Trust deed?'

Without change of expression, Rachel said, 'Here, we have it with us.'

Mordecai stood up, and lunged to grab the document. 'You cannot tamper with the documents of the synagogue and the Trust.'

'Nor can you allow them to be eaten by white ants in the storeroom of the synagogue and nor can you sell a house of prayer for your own gains,' answered Judah quietly.

Mordecai stood up to leave. 'Is that why you invited us, to insult us?' he shouted.

Jhirad understood the seriousness of the situation. 'Sit down Mordecai, this is not an insult. It is the truth. I feel at last someone has woken me up from a long sleep. I will have to understand everything all over again.'

Mordecai retorted, 'You can go ahead and understand all that you want to. As far as I am concerned, I am leaving right now. Mr Chinoy has paid me the signing amount and he will pay me the rest in a few days. So forget the synagogue. It was mine and I had every right to sell my property. Anyway what use is it to us? Would I ever do anything wrong? All my life I have selflessly worked for the good of the community.'

Rachel smiled. 'What community? Where is it? I assume that is the very reason you have sold our house of prayer, isn't it?'

Judah was amused that Jhirad was intoxicated and infuriated. Jhirad said, 'Mordecai, you have cheated everybody. Rachel sister is right. If you are going to Israel, you have to give me in writing that you are resigning from the committee.'

'I was never a member of the executive committee.'

'Yes, you were,' said Jhirad. 'You were appointed in the mid seventies. Since then we have not done anything. It will take me months, but I am going to set the record right with the help of our young lawyer,' he said, looking at Judah, 'and, if Mordecai agrees to give us his resignation, we can call a meeting at this very moment with a quorum of four members and make Judah a member of the committee with immediate effect.'

Mordecai was so angry that he asked for a sheet of paper to write down his resignation. Politely, Judah offered him paper and pen. Quivering, Mordecai wrote a quick two-line letter of resignation and left it on the table.

Before he could change his mind, Judah took it away, read it aloud, folded it and put it away in his briefcase. Mordecai was fuming and fretting as he prepared to leave. He stopped in his tracks when he heard a car stop at the gate. Brownie was barking and Judah went to open the door and returned with Satish Chinoy.

Kavita was surprised to see her husband. He had apparently left in a hurry as he had not even stopped to change and was dressed in his shorts, tee shirt and sports shoes.

Satish Chinoy shook hands with everybody and accepted a drink. Then, addressing Mordecai, he said, 'I hope you are not leaving. I am glad we met. Kavita had told me that you were going to be here. I wanted to speak to you about the land you tried to sell me as your own. I believe it originally belonged to the Dandekars. I am told there is a khat, which is in the name of the Dandekars.'

He turned to Rachel and apologized. 'Madam, excuse me for barging in like this, unannounced. I hope I am not spoiling the party,' he said, with a twinkle in his eye as he looked at Mordecai. 'I had to meet you as soon as possible. I just want to inform Uncle Mordecai that I cannot possibly purchase the land he was trying to pass off as his own. I am a religious man and will not go against the will of God, yours and mine.'

FISH CURRY IN RED MASALA

Ingredients: pomfret, oil, fish masala, red chilli powder, cumin powder, turmeric, coconut, garlic, fresh coriander, vinegar, salt

Method: Cut pomfret into seven pieces, salt and keep aside. Make masala with one teaspoon garlic paste, one teaspoon ready-made fish masala or half teaspoon each of powdered red chilli, turmeric and cumin, with a glass of coconut milk. Mix well and keep aside.

Heat one tablespoon oil in a casserole, add masala, bring to the boil, add fish pieces and cook till done and the curry has a bright-red colour. Garnish with fresh coriander leaves. Serve hot with rice.

Optional: Add a teaspoon vinegar when fish is done and cook for five more minutes on a slow fire.

When Mordecai left, Rachel, who had never once moved from her chair, had a victorious smile on her face. She listened attentively as Jhirad, Satish Chinoy and Judah made plans for the synagogue and decided to regularize the Trust. Rachel felt avenged and satisfied with the turn of events. It was getting late. Jhirad, Lael and Joseph thanked Rachel for her hospitality and left for Bombay.

At last, Rachel's heart warmed to Satish Chinoy and she asked him to stay back for dinner. He accepted her invitation, apologizing for having hurt her by making a deal with Mordecai.

With the help of the younger women, Rachel made a simple fish curry and rice. They still had some leftover kheema patties and mutton chops.

As the moon rose over the sea and they ate together like a family, Satish Chinoy told them how he had had a change of heart that evening.

'I had a strange but mystical encounter, a divine one,' he said, shaken by the experience.

'It happened between six and seven, an hour which always appears suspended in time. A thin line between day and night, when darkness descends on earth. I call it my six o'clock syndrome. When in Bombay, I tide over this period with work, but in Alibaug I go jogging in the garden.

'I am a religious man,' he said. 'In fact both of us are,' he added, indicating his wife. 'I believe in the existence of a supreme spiritual power, which we call God. I have a small Krishna temple at my homes in Alibaug and Bombay and every morning I spend an hour there, before I start my day. Janmashtami is a big celebration in our house. I also respect other gods, and godmen often stay in our home in Bombay.

'After work today, I settled down on the lawn with a cup of tea. I was restless and started reading a book, which I had started some four years back and hadn't gone beyond page ten. I could not concentrate and was feeling low. So I sat staring at the evening star and inexplicably felt peaceful. So I picked up the book and started reading and surprisingly I could concentrate and quietly read up to fifty pages.

'Normally, in Alibaug, I do not like to be disturbed at this particular hour. When it passes, I have a peg of whisky before dinner and retire early with a book or watch a movie on television, something I can never do in Bombay. That is one reason I like to escape to our Alibaug house.

'Suddenly I felt something was happening around me. I was engrossed in the book, but sensed that the temperature had dropped and there was a cool breeze around me. My body relaxed, I felt light and weightless, as though somebody had lifted me and I was suspended in mid-air. It was a good feeling and I assumed it was because of the rural setting. But I knew I was not alone. I felt watched.

'I looked up and saw a man astride a horse, standing right in front of me on my very own lawn. I was furious but, even before I could shout for the chowkidar, I felt I had lost my voice.

'The cavalier was an old man. I had never seen him before. I wanted to invite him for a cup of tea. But he appeared distant. There was something about him that seemed to freeze me into silence, the sort of silence one feels while meditating.

'In the half-light, I saw that the horse looked as if he were carved out of marble. And the cavalier looked like an equestrian sculpture. I looked around to see if the light was playing tricks on me. Was it illusion—because of overwork had I started seeing shapes in shadows? But there was nothing. The truth was that this old man appeared to be real.

'The only sign of life in this statue were his eyes. He was looking at me and I felt hypnotized.

'Slowly my vision cleared and I saw that he was wearing a strange dress. I assumed he was a holy man passing by, so I invited him to join me and offered him a chair. I could not figure out how he had passed my vigilant chowkidars. Perhaps he had mesmerized them and entered the house. Even before I could blink, he was standing in front of me and I was sure I had not seen him move.

'He was standing, leaning against his white stallion. In fact he looked much taller than a normal human being. If he was built like a Titan, the horse was also an enormous animal. The type you see in the European countryside. The animal was twice my height, with a great neck, a silky, smooth mane, a graceful body and an enormous rump. It was harnessed with gold trappings.

'The cavalier was wearing a purple silk robe held at the waist with a plaited red cord and a blue shawl. He was wearing gold sandals and his hair stood around his head like a halo of silver flames. I was fascinated. For a moment, I was worried—what if he was an impostor? My doubts disappeared when he sat down on the chair next to mine.

'I folded my hands and asked, "Guruji, where do you come from, the Himalayas?"

'He shook his mane, but did not speak.

'"You have a magnificent horse. From where did you get him? Looks like an Arabian," I said.

'He smiled affectionately, but said nothing. "Have you taken an oath of silence?" I asked, not knowing what else to say.

'His lips moved, but I did not understand a word. The words were soft like the paws of a lion, walking in the wild. I could not understand what he was saying—perhaps he was speaking in a language I did not know, so again I asked, "Guruji, where do you come from?"

'He lifted his hand, the sleeves fell backwards and he pointed towards Sagav. Then his hand moved towards Danda. I felt he was pointing towards the synagogue.

'Actually, he looked like Michelangelo's painting of God in the Sistine Chapel, you know the one of God flying in the sky and breathing life into Adam. Kavita and I were there three years ago. I realized he looked very much like a biblical character, like someone from the film *Ten Commandments*. Come to think of it, he did remind me of Charlton Heston. As I turned to look in the direction he was pointing, I found myself thinking about Mordecai for no reason at all.

'I felt strange, my body went cold, my heart was beating wildly, and I was perspiring as though my blood pressure had shot up. I turned to look at my guest, but there was nobody there. He had disappeared with his stallion. All I could see was an aura around the chair, it resembled a full moon.

'One moment he was there and the next not there. Slowly the halo merged into darkness. I knew it had been a spiritual visitation. For full fifteen minutes I did not move—I did not wish to disturb the spiritual experience.

'I stood up like one in a trance and called the chowkidar and asked him if he had seen anybody enter or leave the house. He looked at me as if I was crazy. Nobody had either entered the house or left, even the cook who cycled down every evening to buy bread had not yet left the house.

'I walked towards the house feeling light-hearted and happy. And guess what? As soon as I went into the study to look for my cigarettes, I saw Mordecai's file on the table. I was sure I had not left it there. Every evening when my secretary leaves, she sees to it that all important documents are kept in the locker. I flipped through the papers and felt Charlton Heston was telling me not to go ahead with the deal.

'At that very moment, I decided to cancel the deal. The signing money I had given Mordecai was of no importance. Instead, I could feel a hand leading me towards my car and the next thing I knew I was driving towards your house. Kavita had mentioned that Mordecai was at Aunty Rachel's house with the committee members and I had to tell him right away, here in their presence, that the deal stood cancelled.'

Rachel was listening attentively and knew that it was the handiwork of the Prophet Elijah, but did not say anything.

She noticed Satish Chinoy staring at a frame on the wall, his body shaking with emotion. 'Guruji looked exactly like that person in the picture—who is he?' he asked.

'The Prophet Elijah,' said Rachel calmly and asked Zephra to light a candle and pour some wine in the special Passover goblet kept aside for Eliahu Hannabi.

She knew, tonight he was among them.

MIRI CHA MAAS

Ingredients: mutton, onions, garlic, ginger, black pepper, salt, oil

Method: You need half a kilogram cubed goat meat. Wash, salt and keep aside.

Roast two big onions on a skillet or in the oven. When done, cool, peel and make a paste in a mixer with the pulp of onions, ten flakes of garlic and one-inch piece of ginger.

Mix the meat well with the onion paste, add half a glass of water and cook in a casserole or pressure cook till done.

Heat a tablespoon oil in another pan, add cooked mutton, salt, a teaspoon powdered black pepper, preferably freshly ground, and cook till gravy thickens.

Serve hot with a loaf of bread, chapattis or khichdi.

❧

Unlike most curries, which are red in colour, miri cha maas, or mutton in black pepper sauce, is greyish black, like the sky on the night of the shipwreck.

With Mordecai's resignation everything seemed to fall into place. Among the old synagogue documents, Judah found an ancient register of meetings held by the committee. He collected some more information from Jhirad and others and created a semblance of order in the maze of papers. With Mordecai's letter of resignation in hand, Jhirad called an emergency meeting and appointed Judah as a member of the synagogue committee. At the end of the day, Judah was tired with the endless investigations of the old documents and the making of new ones.

A small hitch came their way when Jhirad remembered that Judah would have to first become a member of Danda's Itzraeli synagogue. At first, Judah bristled, but went through the procedure, as his desire to help Rachel was more important than his own discomfort. The membership also meant acceptance from the Jewish community, although Judah was rather sceptical about the whole procedure. Going through the tattered documents, he tracked down all the false documents Mordecai had made. These were kept aside and the committee decided to charge Mordecai with a fine on the grounds of fraud and forgery. Mordecai had already migrated to Israel and they kept the fake documents in a separate file, just in case he ever returned to claim the land he had tried to pass off as his own.

Once the books were in order, Zephra and Judah arranged them in the storeroom cupboards of the synagogue. Except for the cracks in the wall and flaking paint, the synagogue was neat and clean, almost in readiness for the services.

Rachel returned to her old rhythm of spending her afternoons at the synagogue.

Raighad Times, the local newspaper, carried a profile on her with a photograph. They wrote about her dedication to the synagogue and her efforts at preserving the heritage of the Jewish community in Alibaug. For the photo session, Rachel wore a black salwar kameez suit. She also insisted that they shoot the photograph inside the synagogue. Rachel had become an overnight celebrity and was enjoying the attention she was receiving.

The salwar kameez suit had been a gift from her second son, Jacob. That was when he was still a bachelor. On vacation after his army service and before joining the university for a bachelor's degree in computers, he had spent a month with his mother. Rachel had noticed that he had changed and did not feel like eating methi like before; instead he kept asking her to make mutton in black pepper sauce. But whenever she planned to make it, he refused, saying he was unwell, and all through his stay, survived on plain dal and rice. Like all mothers, she fumed and fretted, but knew that she could not ask a direct question and had to find ways to know what was bothering him. She also knew that questions about his personal life annoyed him.

It had been easier with Aviv. When he returned from Israel for the first time, after his army training and before joining his first job as one of the security personnel at Ben Gurion airport at Lod, she had asked him if he wanted to get married.

Casually he said he did, but hadn't met the right girl, unaware that his mother had already made a list of prospective brides.

The first girl he agreed to consider was Irene, his mother's best friend Rubybai's niece. She was working as a schoolteacher in Bombay. He liked her, but hesitated, as she appeared to be tall, in fact taller than him. Her height bothered him. So when his mother asked him if he liked her, he gave her a blank look. She was sure he did not like her. Rachel was disappointed, as she had assumed that Irene was the perfect bride for Aviv.

Irene was taller than most Bene Israel girls, was fair and had a round face, a ready smile, a full figure and soft hands. Rachel was certain Aviv would be happy with her. But on the way back to Danda in the autorickshaw, all he said was, 'She is too tall.'

'Nako or what?'

'Okay.'

'What okay? Marriage is a matter of life and death. If she is okay, then you did not like her.'

He went red in the face and smiled. His mother understood. 'I guess the meaning of okay is that you like her, but are worried about her height.'

'Yes, we would make an odd couple if she is taller than me.'

'How do we find out how tall she is? Shall I call Rubybai and ask?'

Aviv was embarrassed.

Rachel teased. 'Perhaps you should both stand together and we will decide who is taller, Irene or you.'

'Come on Mama, this is no laughing matter.'

'No, I am not joking.'

'I refuse to go through the height-test.'

'But if she was not as tall as the third part of a toddy tree, would you still like her?'

'Sort of . . .'

'You are talking as if we are buying vegetables.'

'Mama, what do you want me to say? I like her, but . . .'

'Okay, when we see them again, you look carefully and make sure if she is taller than you.'

'Are we meeting them again?'

'Yes, next week there is a malida at Rubybai's place, so just stand next to her and find out for yourself.'

'I am not coming to the malida. I get bored. The women stand on one side, the men on the other. How do you expect me to speak to her? So hard, don't you know?'

'Yes.'

'Besides that, even if I smile at her, everybody will assume we are engaged. Jokes apart Mama, before we make sure about her height, the point is, does she like me?'

'Yes . . .'

'How do you know?'

'Because Irene has given her consent, and now they are waiting for your reply.'

'Irene likes me?' Aviv was surprised. 'Look, I am not tall, dark and handsome. I am of medium height, perhaps shorter than her. I am simple and, like a passport photograph, I have two ears, two eyes and a nose. I am healthy, I have a balanced head, a simple lifestyle and a steady job. How boring—she couldn't possibly want to make her life with me.'

'She does.'

'Mama, let's not talk about it. I am not sure . . .'

'You mean . . .'

'Nothing, Mama I do not want to talk about it.'

'Is there somebody else in your life, in Israel?' Rachel asked suspiciously.

'If there was, do you think I would have allowed you to choose a bride for me?'

'I have other girls in mind, in Thane, Bombay, Ahmedabad.'

'Nako,' smiled Aviv.

'Why, because you like Irene?'

'I don't know.'

The matter of marriage came to a standstill and Rachel left the matter in the hands of the Prophet Elijah. And, as they say in the Talmud, help comes in many ways.

A week before Aviv's departure, Rachel was dozing on the verandah and Jacob was watching the news on the television, when they heard a car stop at their gate. Brownie started barking and Rachel woke up and saw Irene and Rubybai rattling the wicket gate.

Jacob was spread out on the drawing room floor, bare chested and dressed in shorts. As soon as he heard them he disappeared into his room. He did not want to be caught in an awkward situation.

Rachel welcomed her guests; it was obvious they were there on a mission. Rachel entertained them and kept the conversation flowing, offering them cold drinks and karanjias. Irene looked nervous, and Rachel tried to put her at ease by talking about dogs and ducks.

Obviously, Rubybai did not want to waste time and asked casually, 'Has Aviv left for Israel?'

'No,' replied Rachel, plucking at her sari and wondering how she was ever going to get Aviv out of his room. 'He must be somewhere in the house,' she continued half-heartedly, 'you know how hard these boys work in Israel, so when they come home all they do is eat and sleep. Must be sleeping.'

Rubybai was unperturbed. 'Good, he is still here. I was wondering if he could take a sari for my daughter Sarah.'

Rachel was worried and not sure how Aviv would react, so she said, 'I will ask him to phone you.'

Rubybai was undaunted. 'I must know as soon as possible, because I have to get it dry-cleaned and the zari needs to be polished,' she said.

Defeated by Rubybai's enthusiasm, Rachel dragged herself to Aviv's room. He was sprawled out on his bed with a magazine thrown over his face. She knew he was awake.

'Aviv,' whispered Rachel, 'Rubybai insists on seeing you before you leave. She wants to know if you mind carrying a sari for Sarah.'

'Tell her I will take the sari. I hardly have any baggage. But I am not getting out of my room. Tell her I am sleeping.'

'She insists on meeting you. Why don't you just come for a second. Don't stay long. Tell her you have a headache.'

Aviv sat up, cursing the day he agreed to even consider Irene as a possible bride. 'Listen Mama, this is going too far . . .' he warned. 'I refuse to fall into this Ruby-Booby trap.'

'Please Aviv, come out for a second,' she pleaded. 'After all, she is my best friend.'

'Yes,' smiled Aviv. 'She also blackmails you. I will just get dressed. Tell me, what shall I wear? A tuxedo?'

'Nothing,' smiled Rachel.

'You are sure, nothing?'

He hugged his mother and, posing like a body builder, whispered in her ear, 'This is the best way to meet a girl. What say you, Mother?'

'Agreed,' she smiled, as he pulled on an old tee shirt and followed his mother to the veranda.

Rubybai hugged him and he smiled at Irene. She did not smile back and looked uncomfortable in the straight-backed chair.

He stood leaning on the veranda wall, asking her, 'Do you have a day off or something? I don't even know what date it is. Whenever I come home, I lose all sense of time.'

Irene relaxed and told him about her school, the children and how she hated giving so much homework to her wards. Soon they were comparing notes about the education system in India and Israel. Not once did Irene get up from her chair and Rachel hoped that the young lady would stand up at least once, so that Aviv could make sure about her height.

But Irene sat in her chair, looking beautiful in a stylish beige salwar kameez with a blue printed dupatta thrown over her shoulders. For the first time, Rachel noticed that she wore a tiny nose ring and had also pierced the rim of her ears. The jewellery suited her. But Rachel was disappointed that nothing on earth could make her stand up. She seemed comfortable in her chair as she crossed her long legs and did not appear to be in a hurry to leave.

Rachel and Rubybai noticed that both Aviv and Irene were talking and laughing like old friends, when Aviv threw all caution to the winds and asked, 'You are really tall for a Bene Israel girl. What is your height?'

'Guess,' she challenged, looking at him coquettishly.

'Five seven?' he asked.

'Five eight.'

'Good,' blurted Aviv, 'I am five nine.'

Unconsciously, Aviv had just proposed to Irene, and, before he could change his mind, Rubybai asked seriously, 'Shall I send the driver for a box of pedas?'

If it had been so simple with Aviv, it was not the same with Jacob. From the very beginning, it was understood that he would find his own wife and he did. But before he found her, there had been many hurdles. The first hurdle was Jacob himself. He was confused from the very moment he saw Ilana at the Tel Aviv beach: he did not know how he would ever get close to her.

He had always been a good swimmer, even when he was in Danda. And when he was posted at the army headquarters in Tel Aviv he often went to the beach for an early morning swim. It was then that he noticed her jogging on the beach.

She was wearing shorts and a tiny tee shirt. Her blonde hair was streaked and tied in a band. She was short, plump, had strong legs, a longish face, a prominent lower lip and enormous breasts. But he could never figure out the colour of her eyes. She had a wheatish complexion and that was one reason he felt she was Indian, but he was not sure, as many Israelis looked like her.

And considering they always bumped into each other at the same place and the same time, he assumed she was living nearby and so, whenever he was in Tel Aviv, he made sure that he was at the beach around six in the morning. He wanted to get closer but did not know how. It looked impossible, as he was falling in love with this beautiful girl.

Jacob continued chasing her for three months till one day he did not see her after his usual swim. He did not want to return to the barracks till he had seen her. She had become a habit. He spread out his towel, lay down in the sand, put on his shades and waited, just in case she was late or had left early, or perhaps she was sick. What if she was a tourist and never returned?

The sun was getting hotter, the beach was crowded and he dozed.

When he woke up, he saw her emerging from the sea with a tall, blonde girl; they were both topless and looked like water nymphs. He could have kept on watching her for ages. She was wearing a white bikini; her breasts were lighter in colour and they stood out from her body, bra-shaped and beautiful.

Since he had come to Israel, he had known many girls, seen innumerable topless women at the beach. She was not the most beautiful woman on earth, yet there was something about her that attracted him. Possibly because he had decided that she was Indian. His eyes followed the two girls till they chose a spot on the sand, spread out their towels and lay down.

He dreamt about her, hoping some day he could rescue her from goons or sharks or a tsunami. She would then cling to him, thank him and kiss him. His head was full of cinematic possibilities. He closed his eyes and dozed, cursing himself for not being bold enough to stand over her and say, Shalom, I am Jacob. I would like to make friends with you. His bunkmate Moshe had a way with girls; if he liked someone, he just walked up to her, spoke to her and started an easy banter. Sometimes it worked; sometimes it didn't. Perhaps he should ask Moshe for help; then he chickened out—what if she took a liking to Moshe? He did not want to take a risk.

He was anxious and worried—what if she had a boyfriend or was engaged to be married? He was disappointed that she had not yet noticed him. He was just a faceless young man on the beach.

Jacob was so obsessed with this beautiful woman that he could not concentrate on anything else. He mused, at least they had one thing in common and that was the time they chose to work out on the north side of the beach. Perhaps they were fated for each other or why else did she catch his eye among the thousands of bathers and joggers on Tel Aviv beach?

After a year, the Prophet Elijah suddenly smiled upon Jacob. His aunt Noreen, who lived in Beersheba, invited him to the yearly Indian festival of dance and music. He often spent his weekends with them, basking in their affection, gorging on home food and watching Hindi films on the video.

Unlike Rachel, Noreen was tall and big-made, wore floral polyester saris and worked in an aircraft factory; Jacob was never sure what she was doing there. Her husband, Cyril, was employed in a hotel near the Dead Sea Salt Works and they lived a comfortable life in a small flat. They did not have children, lived an orderly life and if it hadn't been for the festival, they would have spent the whole day watching Hindi films. The venue of the festival was a huge hall rented by the association of Indian Jews. Jacob thought he was back in India, with the mixed fragrance of curry and perfume. The women and girls were dressed in saris, salwar kameez suits or ghaghras with tons of gold jewellery.

The men were dressed in suits or pathanis. Jacob was the only one dressed in a kurta pyjama with a Gandhi cap, for effect. Unlike his brother, Aviv, who preferred western clothes, Jacob often wore kurtas, sherwanis and pathanis.

The festival started with a Bharta Natyam recital, followed by a series of filmy song and dance numbers. As a finale, the compere announced that the famous singer Ilana Stein was among them with her band led by Samuel Kehimkar. The crowd applauded, and Noreen told him casually that Ilana's mother was a Bombay Jew and her father an Israeli. 'She is a very talented girl. You may not remember, but Samuel used to play the sitar for Raj Kapoor's films,' she said with a certain pride in her voice.

Jacob had seen Ilana so many times in his dreams that he immediately recognized her as the girl on the beach. He gasped, and Noreen asked, 'Are you all right? You look sick.'

He just shook his head and sat frozen in his chair.

Ilana was wearing a flared multicoloured ghaghra, a silver-coloured hanky-choli with a choker and a transparent star-spangled dupatta which covered her bare shoulders. Her hair was piled on her head and caught in place with a tiara. She was wearing bangles up to her elbows and silver anklets over her stilettos. In the bright lights he saw for the first time that she had blue eyes.

He admitted later that when he saw her on stage all decked up she looked too filmy; he liked her better on the beach. So he sat back disappointed, not expecting too much from his imaginary love affair.

But when Ilana started singing, he sat up, spellbound, as he listened to the throaty, sexy voice, which immediately spoke to him. She regaled the audience with songs she had written. As Samuel played the sitar, the tall blonde he had seen with her on the beach played the flute and another musician played the tabla.

Ilana's songs were a fusion of Indian classical music and Israeli folk tunes mixed with Hebrew and Hindi words she had picked up from popular Bollywood numbers. Her body moved provocatively, hands playing with the dupatta, and she used her silver anklets to great effect by picking up the edge of her ghaghra and tapping her heels. With each number, she received a resounding applause and towards the end, as the tempo increased, the crowd went wild, clapping, dancing and asking for more.

Jacob was the only spectator who never moved even once from his chair. He was depressed, because he was certain that he could never reach her. She was a star and he was merely a young, faceless soldier.

That evening he did not have the courage to go near her as autograph seekers crowded around her. Jacob stood at the bar, having ordered a double whisky to steady his nerves, when someone tapped him on the shoulder. It was Ilana.

He could have fainted, was he hallucinating? His heart was beating and he was sure it was a mistake. Perhaps she was speaking to someone else. So he looked over his shoulder. There was nobody, and she was speaking to him.

At a close range, she was even more beautiful. There was a smile in her sea-blue eyes and for a second he wanted to believe that she had noticed him on the beach. But then he realized that she was not interested in him, but in his Gandhi cap, and was asking in Hebrew if he had bought it in Israel. Crushed, he mumbled 'no' in Hebrew and asked, 'I am sure you speak English?'

'Yes,' she spoke in a heavily accented English, 'of course, I speak English and a little broken Hindi. You know, my mother is from Bombay. I like the cap you are wearing, looks very stylish. What is it called?'

'Gandhi cap,' he said, and introduced himself, offering his hand, 'I am Jacob.'

As they shook hands, she was still gushing, 'As I was climbing down from the stage, I saw your cap. I am desperately looking for one. Where do you think I can find it? Perhaps in Lod or Dimona? I want to wear it for my next show. Actually I have a dress with which this cap would make the perfect combination. It is a purple shervani and if I have a cap like this, on stage, it would have the sort of effect I want. Can I have a look at it?'

Enthusiastically, Jacob took off the cap and offered it to her. 'If you do not mind accepting it, I will be very happy to give it to you.'

At first she demurred. 'No, no, not really, I was just asking, I cannot take it. It is just that I am crazy about all things Indian. But, unfortunately, I have never been to India. The cap looked so striking and different in the crowd that I had to speak to you.' Then she pulled off her tiara and her hair tumbled over her shoulders as she looked into the bar mirror and arranged the cap on her head. Jacob adjusted the cap for her, giving it the correct angle and said, 'Please keep it as a gift from me. It looks very good on you. My mother can always send me one from Danda.'

'Danda, where is that?'

Before he could answer and invite her for a drink, a crowd of admirers was standing around them, wanting to shake hands with her and asking for autographs. To add to the confusion, her tall, blonde friend suddenly appeared and asked her to hurry up— they had a late-night recording in Jerusalem. Quickly she thanked Jacob and started moving towards the door. Before Jacob could exchange phone numbers or any other details, she was gone.

As he watched her disappear from his life, all he could see was his Gandhi cap bobbing in the crowd.

ROASTED TONGUE

Ingredients: tongue of goat, salt

Method: Roast two tongues of goat on open wood fire or in an oven. Peel off skin, cut tongues into cube-size pieces, sprinkle salt lightly and serve as a snack, as a bite with drinks or as an accompaniment to curry and rice.

❧❧

That was the year Jacob returned to Danda. Rachel was distraught, as he was always in a bad mood. She hated his silent spells. Normally he would be scooting around between Bombay and Alibaug, going to the cinema or meeting old friends. Rachel did not know how to amuse him. She was worried that he was not even in a mood to eat methi. She had decided to make him speak at all costs. So a week before he was to leave, she cooked mutton in black pepper sauce and roasted tongues of goat, because, besides methi, those were next on his list of favourites. Her recipes would loosen his tongue.

Jacob was touched by his mother's concern and opened a bottle of red Carmel wine. He saw that Rachel had spread out her favourite tablecloth on the dining table with her best plates and goblets. It meant she wanted to speak to him. He prepared himself for his night of revelations.

The food was delicious. Slowly with each morsel he told Rachel about Ilana. Jacob was also worried that Ilana was not like them, and perhaps Rachel would not like her. She wore smart western clothes and was sometimes topless at the beach. Above all, she was rich and famous. Rachel was a trifle worried and so asked him to visit the graves of the ancestors, offer roses there and spend a day at Eliyahu Hannabi cha tapa. The Prophet would show him the way.

He did exactly as she said, just to please her. Not that he believed the Prophet would solve his problems. Even when they were children, Rachel had the habit of making them feel stress-free about exams and results by telling them stories about the Prophet Elijah.

It worked. The day before Jacob's departure, Rachel had a solution for him. He was whistling and mending the poultry house for her, when she asked him, 'Did you say Samuel the sitar player is one of her musicians?'

'Yes.'

'Do you know we are related?'

'How?'

'His wife is a distant relative.'

'Whose side?'

'My side, from Ahmedabad. You know we are all related somewhere or the other. Just go and meet him and one thing will lead to another.'

'How?'

'Very simple. When you phone him, he will invite you for dinner. Then, casually, you could talk about the concert and how you met Ilana. Tell him you want to meet her again. Perhaps he will give you her phone number, or arrange a meeting or invite you to their next concert. You could even buy a new cap for her from the khadi shop at Alibaug. Didn't everything start with the Gandhi cap, so why not use it as a good omen? It could be your lucky mascot. Once you meet her, it is up to you how you handle the situation.'

'It sounds easy, but it is not as simple as you make it sound. And Mama, I am really afraid that you may not like her.'

'Why do you say that?'

'She is not like any of the girls you know.'

'So?'

'She even dresses differently.'

'Why, does she go about in knickers?'

'She could.'

'Does it matter?'

'I don't know. I feel she may never fit into our family.'

'You are worrying unnecessarily about family, clothes and all those things, which do not matter in everyday life. It is your Indian upbringing which makes you speak the way you do. But all these things do not matter if you love each other. When a couple lives together these things get sorted out on their own.'

'I cannot make up my mind. I still do not know her.'

'Find a way and decide for yourself. Don't put the carriage before the horse.'

'What about the family?'

'What family? If you are happy we are happy. Zephra will not have any problems with her. I only hope you will advise her to dress properly when she comes to Danda,' Rachel smiled. 'As for Aviv, he is rather old-fashioned, like your father, but Irene will help him adjust to the idea of a different sort of sister-in-law. And about the other relatives, they will gossip for a while, then start showing off how they are related to Ilana Stein Dandekar.'

'She may never change her name.'

'Why?'

'Because, girls like her don't.'

'About that I will have to think. Anyway, with marriage women change.'

'I do not know, because I think she is a very independent and strong-headed girl.'

'Does that mean she will wear the pants in the house?'

'No idea.'

'Can she cook?'

'I haven't got that close to her. I have been watching her from a distance.'

'Where?'

'At the beach.'

'Does she wear anything at all?'

'A little.'

'Ah, you naughty boy,' giggled Rachel.

'Mama, I am not sure if she will agree to marry me.'

'Why do you say that?'

'I know some of my girlfriends in the army do not want to get married.'

'Girlfriends?'

'Yes.'

'Are there Bene Israel girls in the army?' she asked hopefully.

'Yes.'

'Couldn't you make life simpler by choosing a nice Indian girl for yourself!'

'What makes you think Ilana is not a nice girl?' he asked suspiciously.

'I am sure she is. After all her mother is a Bombay girl. But the way you speak about Ilana, you make her sound like a demon.'

'Do I?'

'Yes.'

'That is not true, actually she is a very talented and intelligent woman.'

'And beautiful.'

'Yes, beautiful.'

'But like a dream, you cannot reach her.'

'True, tell me truthfully, will she like me?'

'She will.'

'How do I look?' asked Jacob, pulling in his stomach and showing off his biceps.

'You are well built, tall, taller than your brother. Army training has done you a lot of good and you have taken good care of your body. You are handsome and if you would grow your hair long, you could look like the young Moses in the *Ten Commandments*, like the prince of Egypt, before he grows a beard.'

'Oh Mama, don't joke. Do I look like Charlton Heston?'

'Yes, actually I am paying you such a big compliment. Can a girl ever refuse a man like you? Till now, she has just noticed your Gandhi cap. Just wait till she notices you, then she will chase you. You never know with women. She may have already noticed you—the cap was only an excuse. I suggest you play hard to get.'

'Shall I?'

'Yes, as soon as you get to know each other, don't run after her.'

'But I am waiting to get close to her.'

'I advise you to give her time and she will respect you.'

'What if she does not like me?'

'That is a possibility and you must prepare yourself for defeat. In Aviv's case from the very beginning we knew that girl and boy liked each other. In your case, it is hard to tell.'

'Isn't it clear that boy likes girl?'

'Very clear, but in case she refuses, what will you do? What if she does not fall in love with you right away?'

'No idea, I am not even sure if I can get that close to her.'

'You never know what will happen. Sometimes love is like magic and if you believe in Eliyahu Hannabi, perhaps your dreams will become a reality.'

Jacob felt comforted and confident. At least he could dare to dream.

Before his departure, Jacob wanted to buy a gift for his mother, something special. That was his way of thanking her. They took an autorickshaw to Alibaug Sari Emporium. As usual she could not make up her mind, so Jacob chose a black salwar kameez suit for her. He thought she would look very good in a Punjabi suit. Rachel was annoyed and asked if he wanted her to wear stylish clothes just because Ilana was fashionable.

'No Mama,' he smiled. 'It is just because I want you to try something new. You know women of your age also wear salwar kameez these days and they look very good. Try it on and see.'

She tried it on, looked at herself and liked what she saw, saying she felt like a teenager. She had never worn anything like that before, nor had she ever worn black.

'Why black?' she asked defiantly.

'Because, after forcing me to eat those roasted tongues and that magical black pepper sauce of yours, you made me feel good.'

Rachel smiled. She did not tell him that she had already phoned Noreen in Israel and asked her to speak to Samuel Kehimkar to arrange a meeting between Jacob and Ilana.

That night, Rachel wore the salwar kameez suit to please him. She felt she had come a long way from nine-yard saris to six, then five and now a salwar kameez dress. She felt free, liberated and happy.

CHIK CHA HALWA

Ingredients: whole wheat or wheat chik, coconut, sugar, almonds, vanilla essence, pink food colour

Method: The Jewish New Year halwa, or chik cha halwa, is made with wheat extract, known as chik. To make the chik, soak whole wheat in water for three days till the grain puffs up. Grind wheat to a smooth paste, spread out in thalis and dry in the sun. When completely dry, chik is broken into pieces and stored in jars.

Ready-made chik is also available in speciality shops in Bombay.

To make two thalis of chik cha halwa, you need about seven litres coconut milk, ten tablespoons wheat chik, fourteen tablespoons sugar, hundred grams almonds, one teaspoon vanilla essence and edible colour, preferably rose pink.

Make a paste with chik and water. Let it stand for four hours. Remove the water which surfaces.

Mix coconut milk and sugar with the paste and
cook on a slow fire, stirring continuously for four hours,
till the paste thickens and leaves the pan. Add vanilla
and colour and cook for another half an hour.

Spread on thalis, cool, cut into diamond shape,
decorate with nuts and serve. Chik cha halwa has to
be eaten fresh as it does not stay for more than two
days.

◆◆

It was Zephra's last night in Danda. She was leaving the next
day. Her visa had expired. She wanted to stay longer, but did
not know how. When she had migrated to Israel, she had given
up her Indian citizenship, not imagining how her life would turn
out.

There was so much to do, so much to organize, so much to
put in order that she did not know from where to begin. Then
there was the wedding, a life to be lived between two countries,
the motherland and the fatherland. One existed in her head, the
other in her heart. She was relieved that Judah was taking care of
the synagogue. He was setting up a charitable trust with the
Chinoys to make a Jewish museum in the synagogue. That meant
collecting Jewish ritualistic artefacts from Jewish homes in India
and Israel, like damaged objects she had seen stored away in
synagogues all over India, cracked shofars, mezuzahs with torn
parchments, old Torah boxes, embroidered curtains of the Ark,
circumcision knives, kosher knives, Passover plates, broken
menorahs, Hanukkah candle stands, and old brass and copper
utensils, which were no longer in use. The list was endless.

Zephra had worked as a volunteer at archaeological sites in
Israel and she was responsible for the collection and classification
of artefacts.

Aviv and Jacob were collecting donations in Israel and the
Chinoys were also writing to many heritage trusts all over the

world. Ilana had organized charitable concerts in Jerusalem and Tel Aviv for the synagogue with a special song she had written for her mother-in-law, Rachel.

Kavita had plans to beautify the land around the synagogue. It was decided that the executive committee of the synagogue and the Chinoy Heritage Trust would work together on the project of preservation of the synagogue.

Zephra's presence was necessary, although she had started feeling the stress since the impossible had become possible and things had started moving ahead. She was finding it difficult to cope with everything. The turn of events had taken her by surprise. She had also applied for fellowships to Israeli universities for the study of Jewish sites in India and had received positive answers. The fellowships would help her live in India.

But when it came to the matter of deciding upon a wedding date, she felt a flutter in her heart, was sick with worry, felt feverish and got goose pimples; her legs turned to jelly and she had frequent attacks of migraine. Yet Zephra had a dream. She wanted to be married in the synagogue at Danda, on the white sands of the beach next to the house, on a full moon night under a canopy of stars, dressed in white and resembling a Chagall painting.

Zephra sighed as she lay on the beach, watching the sunset. The sight always moved her, as it reminded her of her father. He would hold her little hand in his, and they would stand at the water's edge watching the sunset as it changed colour from pink to gold, melting into the deep blue of sea and sky as darkness descended upon Danda.

In the house, Rachel was cooking an enormous dinner for Zephra's departure and keeping herself busy, so as not to think about the hour of separation. Judah was on his way to Danda, possibly still in the catamaran. The Chinoys were sending their car for them to reach the airport in time from the Navi Mumbai expressway. Zephra's bags were packed and there were six more hours for her departure and she was tense.

Far away, she heard a big fish splash in the sea—perhaps it was a dolphin. She also felt she had transformed into one, wanting to swim back into her mother's womb and escape from the confusions of life, home and country. Half awake, half asleep, she smiled, feeling herself floating in her mother's womb.

Zephra opened her eyes and looked at the sky, spreading in endless layers of blues, broken with wisps of clouds and the stark white wings of water birds flying over her, so far, yet so close. She was sure that if she reached out she could touch them. White clouds were collecting around her in a circle, similar to the one she had seen in Marc Chagall's paintings at the museum of modern art in Tel Aviv. For Zephra, at this moment, everything circled around her mother, Rachel, whose smile reflected on her like the silver moon, which had just appeared on the horizon.

In her smile, Zephra saw her own universe rotating in circles, with the ancient synagogue, the houses, the trees, the birds, the animals and the fish.

The sky changed from deep blue to a transparent sheet of glass, just like a Chagall painting, with the bride and groom locked in an embrace, bridging earth and sky. It was a celebration of love.

Rachel and Judah were now the centre of her universe.

They formed the peephole of her universe, through which she could see Israel, India, Danda, the largeness and smallness of life.

In Israel, she was often homesick, dreaming about Danda, a fantasy world, a fragment of her imagination. Then suddenly she felt scattered and afraid, between India and Israel, amid the parachuting figures, the bars of colours like searchlights cutting across her thoughts.

Zephra lay stretched out on the sand between the sea and the house, where Rachel was sprinkling rose petals on the halwa and Judah was reaching out to her from the turbulent Arabian Sea. Soon the El Al flight would take off from Chatrapati Shivaji airport in Bombay and reach Ben Gurion airport in Lod and her dream world would diminish into harsh reality.

Zephra's body was curved into the softness of the sand, but she felt strangely suspended in air. She felt her body make a precarious upward movement, as though she was flying towards the Promised Land, but was rooted to the land of her birth.

Her eyes were wide open as she turned around to see the lights in the house and reconstruct the fragments of memory. Was the house an illusion of the past or a rich bouquet of sepia-tinted images, fragrant, distant and yet very close to her heart?

She trembled, as she saw herself dressed as a bride. There was so much poetry in the white veil flowing endlessly over the sea towards Judah as he leaned over her, kissing her tenderly. She raised her hand to touch him and realized he was not there; instead she was holding a bouquet of flowers. A window suddenly opened in the house with the transparent roof, where the sky bent to veil Zephra the bride, reclining in her groom's arms as he whispered to her, 'My beloved is unto me as a bouquet of myrrh. My beloved is unto me as a cluster of henna flowers in the vineyards of Ein Gedi.'

A door seemed to open in the night sky and in the half light she recognized Judah, standing over her, with open arms, in the land of her lost childhood. For a moment she felt she was drowning in the sifting sands or was she swinging in a cradle of flowers? Again she felt she was rising upwards, her hand grasped firmly in Judah's. They rose and flew above the mundane objects of everyday life towards a home they would eventually make here or there, with fragments from the past, present and future, real and imaginary, merging dreams into reality.

Zephra stood up, feeling better, dusted the sand from her clothes and returned to the house. Rachel saw her from the kitchen, looking drenched and happy. She heard Brownie bark and knew that Judah had also arrived. The table was set with candles, wine and the halwa, pink and fragrant like fresh red roses.

Rachel's heart was heavy as she busied herself in the kitchen, cooking as though it was the New Year. Like the good old days, she would have liked to prepare an offering, a platter with the head of a goat marinated in the spicy herbs of the earth.

But that was for later.

At last, Zephra had decided to get married and it was time to rejoice. Rachel had packed coconut puris for the family in Israel and had spent the whole day making halwa for Zephra and Judah.

It was the perfect recipe for new beginnings.